ANY PORT IN A WAR

ANY PORT IN A WAR

ENEMY OF MY ENEMY BOOK ONE

TIM MARQUITZ   MICHAEL ANDERLE
CRAIG MARTELLE

DISRUPTIVE IMAGINATION

ANY PORT IN A WAR TEAM

Thanks to the JIT Readers

James Caplan
Daniel Weigert
John Ashmore
Mary Morris
Kelly O'Donnell
Peter Manis

If I've missed anyone, please let me know!

Editor
Candy Crum

PROLOGUE

In the bleakness of space, death lurks.

The *Archangel II* sliced through the infinite darkness. Silent, the superdreadnought careened toward the glowing passage of the Zendarin Gate, an out-of-the-way portal off the well-trodden space lanes. Its mission unknown, the *Archangel II* seemed to devour the distance between it and the gate, skirting the nearby asteroid field. Soon, the ship would pass through the gate and disappear, lost to the void forever.

But if ever there was a chance to score a blow against the Federation, against Bethany Anne herself, now was the time.

The *Monger* broke free of the asteroid field it had been hiding in and slipped round the lee side of the gate. The magnetic and temporal distortion, alongside the signal-scrambling river of asteroids, sheltered it from the *Archangel's* scanners. The interference only lasted for a moment, but a moment was all the Wyyvan warcraft needed.

As the Federation ship reached the gate, its nose gleaming in the coalescing energies of the portal, the *Monger* engaged its engines and shields and darted from the whirling shadows of the gate, set on an intercept course.

Bursts of cannon fire erupted from the Wyyvan destroyer, dozens of bolts cleaving through space toward the Archangel's engines with ill-intent. Bright flashes exploded in the view screen. The Federation ship vanished in the glow, and a roar of triumph filled the bridge of the *Monger*.

The *Monger*'s guns spooled up, waiting for the order to fire again as the brilliant illumination flickered and began to fade. The cheers died on frozen tongues as the view screen cleared.

Where the captain of the *Monger* expected to see floating debris and a listing superdreadnought, the *Archangel II* loomed. It was poised threateningly before the Zendarin Gate, barely scratched. Only a charred discoloration against its hull marked the place where the *Monger* had unloaded the whole of its arsenal with all of its ill-intent.

Sirens screamed, breaking the tense silence, and the bridge was suffused in crimson as the *Archangel II* readied its weapons in reply. The *Monger* turned sharp and shot forward, desperate to avoid return fire.

It failed miserably.

The crown jewel of the Federation opened fire, piercing the *Monger*'s shields and punching holes in its armored hull with ease. Vented air billowed frosty into space, spilling from the breaches, and smoke filled the bridge. Warnings shrieked in electronic warbles. One of the *Monger*'s engines flickered and died, and the ship listed, tumbling end over end in the barren vastness, the crew scrambling to right it.

The *Archangel II* continued on its stoic path in silence, entering the gate and triggering the energies within before disappearing a moment later.

The *Monger* drifted without direction, the crew battling for control as the craft hurtled through the darkness, trailing smoke, wreckage, and lives.

CHAPTER ONE

Dirt peppered Taj's goggles with steady *plinks*. The jagged floor of Everon's canyon splayed out below her. Wasn't more than maybe thirty meters away. It whipped past in blurs of green and brown and the occasional lonely yellow.

All it'd take is for my harness to fail to add some red to the palette. A chuckle spilled loose at the thought.

She tightened her grip on the strap lashed to the windrider's hull, the crimped leather of her glove creaking against her palm and settled into the webbing that held her in place. She leveled the flashcannon, balancing it on her shoulder as the power core spooled up.

Deep, throbbing vibrations ran down her arm. She grinned like a madwoman behind the mask that kept the sand from invading her mouth, whiskers twitching in anticipation as she sighted down the barrel.

Taj loved this *gack*.

"Get me closer, Cabe," she whooped into her comm.

"I get you any closer, and you're gonna be eating raw trrilac tail for supper, butt-fuzz and all," Cabe, the pilot of the windrider, the *Thorn*, told her with a raspy laugh, his voice roughened by the nip he constantly nursed on.

"*Mmmmmm*, my favorite." Taj *thumped* her heels against the hull like spurring a horse on.

Cabe sighed into the mic, and the *Thorn*'s nose dipped in response, engines whining as it throttled up. The windrider coughed, once, twice, spitting out billows of black smoke, then engaged. "Hold on. She's a bit sluggish this morning."

"When isn't she?" Taj's hair flailed behind her, ebony tendrils waving like a flag as the ship jolted forward. She howled as the herd of trrilac drew closer, the flashcannon's sensor's beeping at their proximity.

"Careful what you wish for, Taj," Torbon told her. He waved at her from his perch on the other side of the craft. "Remember last season's migration." She could hear the grin in his voice.

He hadn't been grinning then.

"I remember someone squealing like a little girl," Lina said, her voice crackling across the comm. Buried in her tech-cage in the core of the *Thorn*'s engine chamber, if something so tiny could be considered a *room*, her messages were always filled with static, making her sound as if she were light years away. It made her voice cold, robotic; inhuman.

"That someone would be you, Torbon," Taj delighted in telling him. She pointed at him with her eyes, an eyebrow raised, not that he could see it under her goggles.

"How was I supposed to know the trrilac had a ferion

spider sack attached to it? Or that the heat of the cannon would make them hatch?" He shuddered, clearly remembering the moment.

Cabe shrieked, mimicking Torbon. "Get `em off! Get `em off!"

"Hey. You weren't the ones with metallic spiders trying to crawl into your every orifice now, were you?"

The crew chuckled. Taj leaned into her webbing, the straps groaning as she blinked away amused tears. "You should have seen your face."

"Yeah, well—"

The *Thorn* shuddered, engines barking as Cabe eased off the throttle. "Eyes on the prize, folks," he told them. "As much fun as it is to question Torbon's pluck, the herd looks spooked for some reason. Stay sharp."

Taj glanced out over the gathering of trrilac and drew in a deep breath. Despite how many times the crew played shepherd to the flock of strange, graceful beasts, she had to remind herself how dangerous they could be. That's why they were there to begin with.

Though they weren't normally aggressive, in essence, the trrilac were giant, flying, furry, carnivorous whales, and that made them naturally dangerous. Monstrous bodies and sharp teeth were a deadly combination.

Great bulbous bodies trundled through the air, rising and falling with every coordinated flap of the multitude of colossal, membranous wings that trailed down their spines. Wide, round eyes that shone like bright blue moons stared out at the world from above great gaping mouths. Millions of serrated teeth filled their maws, the trrilacs' chewing up anything unlucky enough to cross their path.

Eddies of wind whirled around the creatures, kicking up dust and dirt as they wound their way through the valley that led to the Maladorian Plains.

Home—Culvert City—lay on the other side of those, the town's communal herd of balborans roaming the fields beyond, and the trrilac were headed straight toward the stock. They had done the same every turn for the last twenty turns of the crews' lives, desperate for a meaty meal to see them through the lean winter season. The herd inched closer to the ground with every kilometer.

Taj steadied her flashcannon and eased a finger over the trigger, a claw scraping against the leather of her glove. "Flash in three...two...one..."

She squeezed and fired. The flashcannon *fhwumped*, spitting a glowing ball of light over the heads of the trrilacs. After it passed, it exploded, filling the air with a sparkling wall of brilliant stars, raining down in front of the beasts.

The trrilacs wailed in response, the sound sending goosebumps skittering up Taj's arms. The creatures swayed, bumping into each other, a chain reaction of fuzzy blubber wavering across their hides. The herd held its course, hemmed in place by their cluttered mass and the rocky sides of the valley.

"Firing!" Torbon triggered his cannon, the resulting explosion a bit closer to the trrilacs than Taj's shot was, but again, the creatures held fast, clearly determined not to be swayed from the feast at the end of their long flight.

Taj lashed out, kicking air with a boot, her harness creaking from the motion. "Get along, little woggies."

"Interesting tactic. When explosions fail, try positive thinking?" Torbon chuckled over the comm.

Taj ignored him. "Get us closer, Cabe. These things are as dense as Torbon. We're gonna need another round to turn 'em about."

"Roger that," Cabe called out. The *Thorn* trembled and whined, darting forward with a leap that set the two wranglers swinging in their harnesses.

"Damn, Cabe," Torbon shouted, bobbling his flashcannon as he scrambled to reset himself inside the webbing. "Easy on the throttle."

Taj could almost hear Cabe's shrug from inside the cockpit. "Gears are sandy from last week's storm. She needs a tune-up."

"That's why you call her *Thorn*," Torbon replied, "because she's a—"

"Pain in the ass!" Taj, Torbon, and Lina shouted all at once.

"You're gonna hurt her feelings," Cabe warned, smoothing out the ride. "There. Better?"

"Perfect." Taj watched as the lead trrilac drew closer and closer, its great tailfin slicing through the air a few meters below and whipping up warm currents.

She raised her flashcannon, feeling it prime, and went to squeeze off a shot. That's when something deep inside the *Thorn* rattled. There was a loud *clunk*, then the nose dipped unexpectedly. Taj jolted forward, her harness slamming her into the hull with a thump. The flashcannon went off.

The shot arced downward, striking the trrilac they'd been trailing. The spark detonated with a whistling *squeee*.

The trrilac shrieked and lunged to avoid the heat. Black-ened smoke billowed from a scorched wing that flickered with tiny flames.

"Oh…gack," Taj muttered as the trrilac reared back and rose like a wall before them.

"Hold for evasive action!" Cabe screamed.

"We're gonna die!" Torbon screeched over him, throwing himself against the side of the windrider and clawing at the hull as if looking for a way inside.

The *Thorn* convulsed, and Cabe geared down, dropping them like a stone. Taj's ribs rattled, and her stomach roiled, feeling as though the organ had leaped into her throat. She clamped her teeth against its attempted mutiny. Still, the trrilac tail loomed, filling her wide eyes and leaving room for nothing else. Its shadow washed over her, blocking out the light.

"We're not gonna make it!" she shouted, catching a whiff of roasted trrilac skin through her mask filters. It smelled like burnt rubber and charred fish, and she peeled back her upper lip to try and clear the stench.

Cabe grunted into the mic, but a grinding noise drowned him out. The stubby little wing of the windrider shifted upward as Cabe tried to dodge the flailing behe-moth. It would be too late.

Taj tossed the flashcannon aside, regretting seeing it topple toward the desert below because Gran Beaux had given it to her. She yanked out the viblade sheathed along the outside of her lower leg. A flip of a switch set it to vibrating. The blade became a blur, and she slashed the buckles of her harness away with a couple of quick twists of her wrist. Gravity welcomed her into its arms.

Her legs swung loose, momentum carrying her into a backward swing as the trrilac grew closer and closer. With no time to wonder if what she was doing would work, she waited until her legs were above and behind her, then she yanked hard on the strap—the only thing holding her to the windrider—and let go.

She shot over the top of the *Thorn* right before the trrilac's tail slapped against the side, scraping a trail down the hull where she'd just been. The windrider juddered, and Cabe veered hard to the right at the impact. Taj bounced off the roof, clawing for a handhold that wasn't there, and slid across the smooth hull, careening toward Torbon.

"Heads up, turtle!" she shouted. Torbon popped his head up in time for her to slam into him.

"*Ooof!*" He stiffened as they collided, and she wrapped around him as if she were climbing a tree. She jammed her boots through his webbing to lock herself in place as he swung an arm around her waist to stabilize her. The harness groaned.

The trrilac hurtled past, squealing, its tail catching the short, stubby tail wing of the windrider as it flitted by. There was a reverberating *thump*, and the Thorn spun on its axis. Taj and Torbon's heads clunked together, her goggles and mask pressed into the side of his helmet as the ship rolled over and over.

"I'm *so* gonna be sick," she screamed through clenched teeth, right into his ear. Torbon turned green behind his goggles. She could see his whiskers pinned flat to his huffing cheeks.

"I don't want to die with vomit on me," Torbon shouted,

clawing at the hull. "Or without it, but especially not with it, so we're clear," he squeaked out.

Then there was a jolt, and the *Thorn* righted itself, shuddering to a rumbling hover. Torbon and Taj *thudded* into the hull as the momentum died off.

"I want off the ride, please," Torbon moaned as he gasped in an effort to catch his breath.

"Ain't out of the kettle yet," Taj mumbled, moving her head so Torbon could see the rest of the herd barreling straight toward them.

"Well, ain't that glorious," he groaned. "We're gonna die!"

"Get us gone, Cabe," Taj howled.

The *Thorn* sputtered in reply, lilting a little to the side but not moving.

"Engines are smoked out," Lina's mechanical voice rang out over the comm. "They're not engaging."

Torbon squawked and ducked his head behind the cover of the hull as the herd closed.

"Yeah, like that's gonna save you," Taj muttered, tearing the flashcannon from his stiff fingers. She was surprised he'd managed to hold onto it despite everything.

She spun the barely-charged flashcannon around, using the top of his helmet like a brace to steady the barrel. With only a sideways glance at the dusty gauge that gleamed an ugly yellow, she squeezed the trigger as if her life depended on it.

Because it did.

And not just hers.

The cannon whirred, and an agonizingly long second later, it spit a ball of light. Too close to worry about aiming, the shot struck the first trrilac and exploded against its wide face, blinding it despite its weakened charge.

The beast roared, vibrating Taj's skull, and hurled itself away from the burning ball of illumination. It slammed into its neighbors, knocking them aside and setting the herd to stampeding. Their wails drowned out everything else as the creatures bumped and jostled one another, veering every which way to escape the glittering spark that burned the face of the beast in front of them.

A moment later, the windrider was past, the trrilac herd scattered in their wake. The creatures desperately flapped their wings, millipede legs kicking underneath. They skirted the canyon walls and shot upward in a panic, disappearing over the peaks on either side.

Taj slumped against Torbon, the harness groaning with both of their weights. She cast a quick glance over her shoulder and spied Culvert City in the near distance, the end of the canyon a short distance away. She sighed at how close they'd come to disaster.

"Put us down," Torbon whined.

The *Thorn* hummed and eased toward the ground, landing gear creaking as it deployed. The windrider settled on the sand a moment later with a dull, but satisfying, *thump*.

"Oh, blessed earth," Torbon muttered as he unbuckled his harness. He and Taj tumbled to the dirt, kicking up a cloud of dust. "I'll never leave you again." He caressed the solidness beneath them. "Never."

The cockpit shield buzzed and peeled back, and Cabe clambered out of the ship. He'd already peeled his helmet loose, and wild strands of his dark hair stuck out everywhere. He looked feral, the light bracing of fur dark on his cheeks as he raced over to the pair, spitting out nip juice in a dark stream.

Lina scrambled out a few seconds later, her pale fur smeared with grease. Her uniform was no better, black stains appearing in random stripes across its brown covering where she'd wiped her hands or an errant tool, or twelve. She was shorter than everyone by a head or more, which was exaggerated by her hunched posture from many hours squeezed in the *pit* of the *Thorn*.

Taj shoved Torbon off her, then climbed to her feet. She dusted her uniform off with shaking hands and chuckled at the worried expressions on her crews' faces.

"All's well that ends well?"

"If you consider almost dying a good thing." Cabe shook his head, examining Taj for wounds. Lina hovered behind, doing the same.

"*Almost* being the key word in that sentence," Taj replied with a grin.

"No, I'm perfectly fine," Torbon muttered. "Taj likely gave me a hernia while I kept her from falling to her doom, but I'll be okay. Probably. Don't you worry 'bout me. I might die, but that's cool."

Cabe held a hand out to Torbon and helped him up, patting him on his back to shake the dust loose. "I'll save up for flowers for your funeral. How's that?"

"*Ooooh*, I can make the casket," Lina said, rubbing her hands together. "A mechanoid one that will walk to the hole and crawl inside and bury itself."

"Yes!" Taj shouted, pumping a fist. "That would be so

cool. We wouldn't even have to show up if you did that. We could watch his burial on the holo-screens."

Torbon sighed.

"Maybe Jadie will bake a casserole." Cabe licked his lips.

"You know I hate her casseroles," Torbon mumbled.

Cabe smiled. "Good thing you'll be laid up in your own personal hole and won't be eating any, huh?"

The crew chuckled, and Torbon pulled his helmet off. Taj ran her fingers through the tawny fur on his head, which was pulled back so tight it looked like his tail.

"Aw, don't go gettin' your feelings in a tangle. You did good out there," she told him. "Thanks for the save."

He grunted, but there was a slight flicker of a smile peeling his whiskers back.

Then she caught sight of her flashcannon, lying bent and broken in a heap a distance away, the sun reflecting off its wreckage. "Sweet Rowl, Beaux's gonna swat my ears," Taj said, motioning to the weapon. No amount of adjusting or polishing would make it okay. "Still, could be worse, I guess."

"No doubt about that," Torbon muttered, shaking the dirt from his uniform. "It can *always* be worse."

"Uh," Cabe started, reaching back and tapping Torbon on the arm a half-dozen times in rapid succession, "I'm thinking you two might be prophetic."

"What are you going on about?" Torbon asked.

Taj, Lina, and Torbon spun around as one and followed Cabe's upward gaze. Taj's heart sputtered in her chest.

High above the Plains, breaking through the lower atmosphere, was a great, burning mass. Reddish-orange flames colored the sky as if dawn had come 'round a second time today. Clouds billowed as the massive fireball cut through them and plunged toward the planet. Thunder rumbled overhead, shaking the ground while sparks of electrical current set the crew's fur to standing on end.

"What the gack is that?" Lina asked, voice wavering. The lack of comm static and her excitement made each syllable unusually sharp.

Taj shrugged. "I have no idea," she said," but whatever it is, it's coming down right outside of town! We need to get there."

"Need?" Torbon asked.

"Need," Taj confirmed, darting toward the windrider without waiting any longer.

Torbon sighed loud enough to be heard and followed the others, who had already shot off after her. "I clearly have no idea what the word *need* means," he muttered.

CHAPTER TWO

"Not to sound like Torbon or anything, but are you sure this is smart?" Cabe asked as they hunkered behind a rise.

They stared out at the metallic gray monstrosity that skidded to a halt just on the other side of the Maladorian Plains. It tore a great trough through the dirt and shrubbery for kilometers. Reddish brown clouds lingered in the air, swirling and obscuring their view. Daylight dimmed in its wake.

The balborans mewed uncomfortably somewhere nearby, the herd lost in the artificial dusk. The *Thorn* sat in artificial dusk, hidden out of sight in the tall grass, its engine *tinking* eerily as it cooled.

"Smart? Maybe not. But the right thing to do? Yeah, I think so," Taj answered. Though she'd never seen a starship like the one before them, hissing and groaning as it settled, she knew well enough to understand there'd been nothing controlled about its landing. "Someone could be hurt. They came down hard, and only managed to get the nose up at the last second to keep from snapping the thing in half."

"That's no frigate," Lina warned, her hand cupped over her eyes as she examined the crashed star craft. "I'm seeing what look like turrets poking out of the sand there near the aft of the hull. Maybe some along the starboard side, too, though can't see what's at the foredeck with all the bluster it kicked up. That'd tell me for sure what we were looking at. I'm guessing it's a destroyer."

"And what would you know about destroyers?" Torbon asked.

"Hey! I spent my three turns defense service under Old One-eye. He saw action over Felinus 4 during the Tab Offensive."

Torbon chuckled. "That old Tom ain't seen any action since before Mama Merr squeezed Gran Beaux's litter out in a puff of dust."

Lina stiffened and slapped her arms across her chest. Taj muffled a chuckle. "Maybe not, but he's got a vid-libe of old holos from the war I got to study." Lina bared her teeth and hissed at Torbon. "Those are blast cannons juttin' out from under that wreck, I'm tellin' you." With that, she turned to snarl at Taj, who whipped her hand away from her face, forcing her grin into a neutral expression. "We need to be careful."

"We will be," Taj promised as she inched forward over the rise, prowling closer to the crashed starship. "Just need to be sure."

"There's that word again," Torbon mumbled. "*Need.*"

"I agree with Lina. Maybe we should wait for Beaux and the regulators before we go sticking our noses in burrs." Cabe shook his head. "Plus, I saw some scorch across the hull before it hit. I don't think it was an accident that brought that ship down."

"Of course, you saw scorch," Taj called back. "That tub hit the atmosphere flat on its belly like you did that time Jadie pushed you into the pond. A ship like this hasn't got the deflectors to shunt that kind of burn. For gack's sake, it shouldn't even have broken orbit without a tow-ship guiding it in and an aerial berth to settle in. I'd be more surprised if it *didn't* have scorch."

Torbon went to raise a finger, and Taj spun on him, shutting him up with a glare of her amber eyes.

"And before you ask how I know anything about anything, Lina wasn't the only one who studied the holos during her service turns. Maybe if you and Cabe hadn't been so busy playing with the flight sims or your ships' blasters, blowing up dunes, you'd have learned something useful. Besides, by the time Gran Beaux and the others muster and find their weapons, any survivors on that ship will have curled feet up and gone to Rowl." Taj started forward again, waving the rest on. "Come on, unless you're 'fraid you'll wet your fur."

Cabe sighed and trailed after her with a shrug. Lina followed, shaking her head. Torbon brought up the rear, muttering under his breath about a steel bladder. Taj grinned, front teeth jutting past her lips where the others couldn't see them.

Whatever they thought about the strange ship lying in the scrubland before them, each and every one of them wanted to know who or what was inside as badly as she did. They just weren't as willing to admit it.

Eight insufferably long turns had come and gone since the quartet had served their mandatory tour of duty with the defense forces tasked with protecting their planet, Krawlas, from any and all invaders, a holdover requirement from the old world Gran Beaux demanded of the people. Taj chuckled under her breath. *As if anyone cares about raiding a dirt-poor wasteland like Krawlas.*

Still, it had been the last bit of excitement the group had had, practicing their skills in the three remaining antique freighters that had brought the original survivors of Felinus 4 to the planet, where they'd settled and created the small community of Culvert City.

Outside of their seasonal efforts at redirecting the migration of the trrilac, the last interesting thing Taj could remember happening on Krawlas was when a sparkstorm rolled through unexpectedly, erupting over the fields and sending the balborans scattering, tongues of twisted lightning crackling and setting fire to their tails.

She pushed on with a grin on her face, remembering the panicked herd, as they closed in on the downed ship. At first, she'd thought she'd misjudged the distance, the trip taking longer than expected, only then realizing the scope of what she was looking at as they neared, the ship farther out than she'd realized because of its deceptive size.

It was huge.

Stark gray, with only lighter patches on the hull—and the scorch marks—to delineate one section of the craft from another, Taj realized Lina had been right. This wasn't any kind of passenger or supply ship as she'd hoped.

In a few places where the atmospheric burn, or the crash itself, had pried plates of armor loose, the width of it was exposed, showing it to be as thick as her skull. There was no way the ship was simply some modified freighter, weapons tacked on for show. No, this was definitely a destroyer, a star craft designed for one purpose: *war*.

That realization brought her up short. The shuffled feet of the others sounded behind her, but she thought she'd caught a faint sound in the background, one she couldn't immediately identify.

"What's wrong?" Cabe asked over her shoulder.

She shushed him with a raised hand. Her eyes trailed the lower half of the ship, steam spilling serpentine from unseen ducts. A deep, rumbling groan rose in her ears, and the ground vibrated under her feet. There was no mistaking the sound this time.

"Oh, gack," Lina muttered, pointing at the hull. The barest of lines appeared along what had been seamless steel. Light trickled out as a great slab of the ship pushed forward, separating from the rest and easing toward the ground. A second sound drifted to their ears.

"Wait! What is that? Are those…?"

Stomping boots! Taj finished for him inside her head. *Soldiers.* Her heart fluttered against her ribs as the gravity of their situation fell over her. "We need to go. Now!"

Spurred on by the sharp edge of her voice, the group spun about and ran, kicking up sand and whirls of dust in their wake. But it hadn't been fast enough.

The ship's gangway dropped to the ground with a hiss and a menacing *thump*. Yellow lights split the haze, and Taj knew they'd been spotted right away as a sharp, crisp beam of illumination tickled her scruff, circling around to highlight them in the gloom. A symphony of hums resounded at their backs, triggering a deep-seated memory of something she'd seen in one of the old holo-vids. It wasn't a pleasant recollection.

"Incoming! Scatter!" she screamed, shoving Torbon to the side as she veered opposite.

A greenish bolt of energy tore up the earth between them, peppering the two with shards of rock and charred pieces of twisted scrub. A second blast scorched the air right above Taj's head as they crested a rise and tumbled down the short decline on the other side. Taj caught a shuddering breath and braved a furtive glance to see who chased them. She regretted it instantly.

A dozen aliens stomped toward them, garbed in some strange form of powered armor Taj had never seen the likes of before. A cold chill cascaded down her spine in sharp contrast to the heat of the blast weapons searing the air.

Elongated, bulbous, black-helmeted skulls rose above strange apparatuses that protruded from their faces like snarling wolf muzzles. Hoses ran from both sides, and steam burbled in the tubes with their every breath.

Oblong eyeholes glared back at Taj, green flutters in the glass warning of sight enhancers as the aliens charged across the scrubland, headed directly toward them. Broad pauldrons protruded from their shoulders, exaggerating the width of the tall, gangly creatures. Long, slashing armored tails swung behind them, but it was the gaping abyss of the blaster barrels pointed her way that resonated most with Taj.

These soldiers—these creatures—whoever or whatever

they were, had no intention of capturing her and her friends. They meant to kill them.

"Go, go, go, go, go! Get to the *Thorn*."

Lina bolted but stumbled as the ground leveled a few meters later. Just before her hands touched the dirt, Cabe had her by the collar and yanked her forward, keeping her on her feet. A half-dozen more blasts shrieked overhead as the soldiers squeezed off shots without even bothering to aim. Lina grunted and tore loose, bolting ahead.

"Would now be a bad time to say I told you so?" Lina shouted over her shoulder. "Because, I have to say," she sputtered between gasped breaths, "I really did tell you."

"Run now, be right later," Taj shouted back. Much as she didn't want to listen to Lina's *mrowling* about it, she hoped there *would* be a later.

With the energy bursts exploding all around them, she really wasn't sure there would be.

CHAPTER THREE

Captain Relius Vort stared at the smoking console. His eyes traced the black char where fire had marred the pristine gleam of the equipment and warped the frame and shattered several of the monitors. He fought the urge to lash out, to kick the console until it gave way in a flurry of pieces.

Instead, he stepped back and gave the crewman working on it more space, sucking in a deep breath to settle his nerves. Vort ran a hand across the dome of his skull and immediately pulled it away, hating the clammy, bald flesh he found there. His anger wasn't yet under control.

He'd had his crew hold the *Monger* together with pure fury and willpower after that slag Bethany Anne and her *Archangel II* punched a hole in the port engine core, sending them listing, out of control. They'd made it as far as some off-the-grid gate before the other engine flared from the effort and died, sending them tumbling through the portal without anything resembling control.

Now they were stranded on some backwater planet that had barely registered on their scanners before the *Monger* broke the atmosphere and slammed into the surface.

Vort had delayed sending a distress call to command, dreading the fallout from having failed to bring down the *Archangel II,* despite having stumbled across the ship totally unaware outside an asteroid field.

Worse still, Vort had to report that the Etheric Federation craft hadn't even felt the *Monger* worthy of being finished in battle, choosing instead to swat it as though it were an annoying insect, leaving the ship to flare out and drift off to die in empty space as the *Archangel II* continued on its way as if nothing had happened.

That was the worst part, he thought.

Wyyvan Command would agree, and the longer he could avoid relaying his request for assistance, the better. Even if that meant spending a few extra days on a dirt planet in the middle of nowhere while trying not to break anything else.

He'd sent troops to secure the perimeter of the ship as soon as it had settled, though he didn't expect trouble. KI1047-32—or Krawlas as the local designation stated in the star registry—was a barren, low-tech outpost of a planet. If his ship's orbital scans were correct, the planet was occupied by little more than two hundred souls that were congregated in a tight, geographic location on the small globe.

He glanced at the console again and ground his teeth. A

spark fluttered as the crewman worked, but there was nothing to do but trust the intel to be correct until proven otherwise. His men would have the equipment working soon enough for confirmation.

Or, at least, they'd better.

Until then, he'd secure the crash site and weigh his options.

"Status report," he called out, not even bothering to turn around as he heard the clatter of Commander Dard's sullen boot steps behind him.

"Sir."

The *thump* of the man's fist striking his chest told Vort the commander had followed protocol and saluted despite not having his captain's full attention. Vort smiled at that. It was what made Dard so useful as his second in command. He could be trusted to do what was expected of him.

"We stumbled across a small number of locals outside the ship. They appear to be Furlorians at first glance, though none have been seen in decades. I've dispatched a squad to hunt them down and set an example to the rest of the inhabitants," the commander reported.

Captain Vort only then turned to face the officer. He shook his head. "No. Call the troops back," he ordered. "The natives are no threat to us, and I'd rather the men do damage assessments of the hull than waste time chasing the local fauna."

"Right away, sir." Dard complied instantly, speaking into a silenced comm channel, which allowed him to pass the order along without the captain hearing so much as a word.

"Keep an eye out, of course," Vort continued. "If they gather en masse and head our way, you've free rein to shut them down by whatever means necessary. Until then—"

"Sir!" the crewman at his back called out, interrupting him. "Displays are back online."

Captain Vort grunted and waved Dard back to his station, spinning about to face the damaged console without another thought for the commander, certain his order would be carried out. Flickering screens wavered and *skreeeed* a moment before settling. The ship's data rolled wave-like across the displays before stabilizing. His gaze darted back and forth, taking it all in.

"Make sure the initial life readings are accurate, specifically the population, then scan for any subterranean energy sources that might indicate hidden pockets of locals that might be troublesome or can provide us with supplies." Vort surveyed the consoles, finding reasons to remain on the bridge. "What are the conditions of the engines and flight control?"

"Flight controls remain stable, and we're working on the engines, sir," the crewman answered, swallowing hard afterward. "We're able to lift off and move the ship terrestrially, short distances, but there is too much damage, and we don't have the parts to ever hope we'll be able to escape the atmosphere or reach orbit."

The captain drew in a deep breath and let it out slow, nodding to the man, motioning him to get back to work. Vort had expected as much, but hearing it stated plainly did nothing to better his mood. He was stuck on this damnable planet after his failure, and there wasn't any delaying the inevitable any longer.

"Ready a secure channel to Command, routing it through to my quarters." He didn't want any of the crew to witness the conversation between him and Grand Admiral Galforin, especially considering it would be anything *but* a conversation.

"Captain, you need to see this right away," Dard called out, waving Vort to his duty station as the captain resigned himself to informing Command of their current situation. And while Dard's brusque summons crossed the line into insubordination, Vort understood the man well enough to know he wouldn't have discarded protocol without good reason.

Vort stomped down from the command dais and sidled alongside the commander. Instinctively, he lowered his voice as he asked, "What is it?"

Dard tapped the screen before him, manipulating the display so it cut away sections of information, leaving a single report remaining. Green, glowing numbers and text scrolled before Captain Vort.

"What am I looking at?"

"Toradium-42 deposits, sir." The captain looked closer at the information, seeing now what had the commander so excited.

"Those numbers can't possibly be correct." Vort stiffened, mind reeling.

Commander Dard nodded. "They are. And this is only a surface scan." He glanced about, almost suspiciously, before returning his attention to the captain. "The entire planet is rich with the mineral, sir. The *Monger*'s *landing*—" Vort ignored his subordinates poor choice of words "—dug up a trench filled with enough to power half of Belor Prime for a turn, at least. Deposits begin less than two meters below the surface, and the density of the Toradium-42 makes it impossible to push deeper without inserting a probe for closer inspection."

Captain Vort reached out and squeezed Dard's shoulder as he realized exactly what all this meant. He offered up a wry grin. "Excellent work, Commander." Vort gestured toward the screen with his chin. "Keep this information locked down until I say otherwise. I've a call to make." He spun on his heels, then paused. "Oh, and while I'm doing that, prepare a tactical group. The locals might end up being more of an inconvenience than I'd originally thought given this turn of events." He chuckled and spun about on his heel.

Unlike his first attempt, Captain Vort smiled as he made the walk to his chambers, his steps lighter than they had been in months. He was suddenly far more excited about reaching out to Wyyvan Command than he had been.

While he still had to report his failure to bring down the *Archangel II* and that damned scourge they called an empress, he'd stumbled across something that even the most cynical of Wyyvan Command couldn't deny was a victory.

The means to take the fight to the Etheric Federation on a scale never before imagined.

CHAPTER FOUR

Taj hissed as a bolt of energy ripped a hole in the windrider's hull a handspan from where she clung to Torbon in the one-remaining harness as they fled, the ship rocketing into the air. Char and scorched metal stung her nose, forced into her face by the wind, and she snarled, the scent making her eyes water.

There hadn't been time to slip her goggles or mask back on as they ran from the soldiers, and she was paying for it as Cabe throttled the *Thorn* into a whine and did his best to put distance between the ship and the aggressive aliens.

It wasn't enough.

"Holy Rowl!" Lina screeched, not even the distortion of the comm muffling the worry in her voice. "They clipped the stabilizer core with that last shot," she shouted. "It's blown."

"I'm guessing that's not a good thing," Torbon said between clenched teeth.

"No, it's really not," Cabe howled, the *Thorn* juddering as if to emphasize his words.

The windrider shook as if it were ready to fall apart, then it began to roll sideways. Taj's stomach climbed into her throat, a hairball of epic proportions. "Dog balls," she mumbled under her breath and sank her claws into the strap, desperately trying to keep from slipping loose.

"Hold on!" she screamed.

"What the gack do you think I'm doing?" Torbon screamed as the windrider continued its roll, dangling the pair over the desert floor, the sand and scrub shrieking past below.

Another energy blast hurtled by as the *Thorn* spun, scoring a piece of Torbon's boot heel. He didn't even have time to complain before the two Furlorians were upside-down. Taj saw his face redden as the blood rushed to it and knew hers appeared pretty much the same way…minus the stupid look.

The muscles in her shoulder and back groaned, her fingers aching, as she held on for dear life as the ship continued to spin. A moment later, they *thumped* onto the hull as they reached the apex of the roll.

"We're so gonna die!" Torbon shouted over the wind.

"You said that the last time, too." Taj growled, her gaze darting about, looking for a better way to secure them to the ship before Torbon's oft-stated prediction came true.

"I really mean it this time," he told her as gravity took hold once more, and they started sliding down the hull again.

"We're not dying," she shouted back. "At least, I'm not."

"Wait! What?" Torbon's eyes slammed into the sides of his wide sockets, staring at her.

Taj grinned and punched her arm through the hole in the hull, grateful for the sleeves of her uniform, which kept the heated metal from burning skin, as she sunk up to her elbow before hitting resistance.

"What are you doing?" Torbon shouted.

"Hoping Rowl has some love for a runt and an ugly Tom," she said.

She bent her arm and locked it in place as best she could. Her fingers clasped the inside frame as the windrider dropped out from under them once more, leaving them hanging in empty space, legs flailing.

Taj bit back a scream as the muscles in her arm twanged, catching the whole of their combined weights. Bones creaked in her elbow, and she nearly released the strap to grab her injured limb. Only some deep-seated sense of self-preservation kept her from doing so, reminding her it was a long, long way to the unwelcoming dirt hurtling by below.

Then the *Thorn* shifted again, wrenching her shoulder and nearly ripping it from its socket. This time she did scream, unable to hold back.

Torbon twisted and pulled her in tighter as the windrider leveled a bit, taking enough of the weight off her arm to keep it in place. "We can't do this much longer," he screamed into the comm. "Taj's gonna lose an arm...or worse."

"Stabilizer's on the fritz," Lina called out. "We go down now, here, we go down *hard*."

Cabe growled. "We don't go down now, we'll go down

even harder," he countered. "We don't have a choice. Hold tight."

The ship rolled to where the swinging pair were once again atop it, only the fury of the wind tearing at them, and Cabe killed the engines. The nose of the *Thorn* dipped, and the cockpit windscreen popped open to the right of Taj. There was a sharp *crack*, then a *thud*, as the screen slammed into the hull and tore loose as it was ripped away from the windrider.

"Take the stick," Cabe shouted to Lina as he peeled himself free of his seat and stood upright.

"What the gack are you doing?" Taj screamed, but she knew exactly what the instant the words split her lips. "No! Don't you dare!"

Her warning fell on deaf ears as Cabe raised his arms, letting the howling wind catch hold of the material hanging loosely from under his arms, from where he'd unzipped his suit to create makeshift wings.

There was a loud snap as the material caught the frenzied air, and Cabe was torn from the cockpit. He yowled and tucked tight an instant later, spinning in midair and spreading his arms again, catching the wind once more.

Unable to look away, Taj thought she'd be sick watching his aerial acrobatics, certain he would be flung past, tumbling to his death. But Rowl favors the bold.

And the stupid, it seemed.

Cabe collided with the wing, letting out a wounded grunt. His arms snapped around it like serpentine vices, hands slamming together on the opposite side and locking tight. He hissed through bared teeth, but his clasp held, and he locked his legs around the wing to secure his position.

Taj's breath froze in her lungs as she was certain all he'd done was expose himself to the same danger she and Torbon faced, and soon, all three of them would be little more than smears of fur against the earth. Lina would build robot-caskets for them all, but only if she managed to clamber into the cockpit and grab the stick before the *Thorn* rolled upside-down again and spit her out before she got a chance.

Then Cabe's laughter whipped past Taj, driven by the wind.

"Are you insane?" she shrieked.

"An insane genius," he shouted back, matching her scowl with a feral grin.

And that's when Taj realized the craft had stopped spinning, suddenly comprehending that his weight hanging beneath the *Thorn* was keeping it from swinging around again. As she caught her breath, she dared lift her head to see Lina climb into the cockpit seat and strap herself in with one hand while snatching control of the stick with her other.

"I lost a life watching you do that, Cabe," Lina shrieked from beneath her mask, which she'd somehow managed to slip back on, along with her goggles before taking over piloting duties. "I'm not liking you much right now."

"Get us low and slow enough for us to drop off safely, then eject right after," he told her.

Taj could see the strain beginning to take hold of him. His grin wavered and fell away, and he wormed lower on the wing, his hands inching up the opposite forearm as he sought a better grip to keep himself from falling.

"Quickly," Taj ordered Lina.

As fearless and heroic as Cabe had been, he wasn't going to last much longer while clinging to the wing the way he was. Even with the *Thorn* slowing, there was simply too much wind and gravity to fight, and that discounted how hard Cabe had struck the wing.

Though he hadn't appeared to have been hurt in the collision, she could now see red spilling from between his pursed lips, trailing out behind him as if he were flying a crimson banner from his teeth.

"Idiot," she muttered under her breath, unable to peel her eyes off him. "Get us down, Lina!"

"Working on it."

Torbon groaned as the *Thorn* shuddered again, Lina having triggered the thrust reversers and slowing the windrider even more. Then the craft dipped hard and fast, the ground hurtling toward them.

"Not that fast!" Taj screamed, but if the engineer-turned-unexpected-pilot heard her, she didn't show it.

Brown scruff filled Taj's vision, and she swallowed hard, a knot forming in her throat that kept her from screaming. Still, that didn't stop her skin from crawling with terror as the ground kept coming at them. She hugged Torbon tighter, hearing him mutter underneath her, and closed her eyes.

Then a sudden, snapping whiplash ripped her eyelids open.

"Now!" Lina shouted. "Jump now!"

With nothing more than faith in her friend—and a liberal dose of prayers muttered under her breath to Rowl —Taj did exactly what she was told.

Well, she tried, at least.

She let loose of the strap and kicked away from the hull, feeling Torbon slip out from under her and be taken by the wind. Cabe let go, too, spinning away in her peripheral vision until he disappeared.

Unfortunately, pulling her arm free from inside the hull was impossible. The sleeve, which had kept her from being burned earlier, had decided it didn't have her courage. The melted material had fused to the edges of the hole punched in the side of the windrider, holding her in place.

"You have got to be gacking kidding me! *Now* you want to keep me on you, you damn piece of—"

"I said jump!" Lina shouted.

"Heard you the first time," Taj answered, wildly gesticulating toward her arm. "Bit stuck here."

"Oh…"

"Yeah, oh…" Taj mumbled, peering over her shoulder at the ground, which couldn't have been more than a meter beneath her, hurtling by so quickly that it was a gray blur punctuated with splotches of jagged brown.

She was getting pretty sick of imagining herself splattered across the dirt today.

That thought in her head, she hissed and yanked her arm, hearing the material of her suit tearing but still not giving way.

"You might…uh, want to hurry," Lina warned, drawing Taj's gaze forward.

Ahead, a scruffy dune appeared, it's rocky cluster appearing as if it were shooting up from the ground, rising before them as if it were a monstrous hand, desperate to swat them from the sky.

The hull rumbled beneath her as Lina throttled the

engines up, but they refused to engage, a black puff of smoke spewing out the back as confirmation of their failure. Lina growled, the sound reverberating through the comm.

"Roll over, damn you!"

Taj stiffened, a thought besides her imminent death popping into her skull. "That's it!"

"What's it?" Lina asked.

Taj didn't bother to respond. She twisted, sliding against the hull, and positioned herself so that her feet were beneath her. Her arm twinged with agony, muscles and tendons pulled tight and stretched to their limits.

"I'm about to tip the cradle," Taj shouted. "Pop your belt and get ready."

Lina mumbled something across the comm that Taj didn't hear, but she had to hope her friend had heard and, even more importantly, listened. Without time to question what she planned, Taj shimmied her butt off the hull, in the same direction as the wing Cabe had been clinging to.

Lina gasped, and Taj thought she heard the faint click of the seat restraints coming loose. Agony then tore all sense from her except that of pain. Blackness gnawed at the edges of her vision, drawing it into a tunnel, and she felt something tear at her elbow. Blood splattered across her face, warm and gritty, and the darkness took her, a metallic *crunch* echoing all around her.

To her regret, the reprieve lasted all of a heartbeat.

She came to as she hit the earth, rolling into an uncontrolled tangle of limbs and fur. Sand and scrub filled her mouth, and dust burned her eyes as she tumbled, head over tail for what seemed an eternity. She came to a stop, a jarring collision doing little more than jarring her skeleton about inside her body—which had been to her surprise and delight.

Taj slumped into the dirt, hazy consciousness picking out her surroundings as her head slowly stopped spinning. She glanced about, blinking sand from her eyes, and realized she'd slid into the base of the sand dune, its slope bringing her to a halt.

A blurry glance at her arm told her the wound there was superficial, a layer of skin peeled back and oozing blood, dirt already helping it to clot. She moved her elbow, and, despite a deep ache and the sear of a bad scrape, it seemed fine. It'd be sore for a while, but considering the circumstances, it could have been far worse.

She groaned and pried her eyes open wider and spotted Lina lying in the scrub a few meters in front of her. Her friend stared with wide eyes as she clambered to her feet, wobbling at the effort. Taj groaned at seeing her friend, alive and moving, though she hardly looked stable.

Behind her, Cabe and Torbon stumbled into sight, both sliding to a halt as they spied the two women, alive and somewhat well.

"Oh, thank Rowl," Cabe muttered, falling to his knees in the sand. Torbon came to a halt beside him, bending over at the waist, struggling to catch his breath. "I thought you both were going to die."

"Glad to disappoint you," Lina mumbled, apparently deciding she didn't like standing as much as she liked lying down. She flopped to her back on the ground, kicking up a cloud of dust.

"Me, too," Taj muttered, the words spit loose with mouthfuls of dirt for emphasis. "Me, too."

"Where's the *Thorn*?" Cabe asked, scrambling to get back to his feet, panic in his voice.

A hand rose from the dust and waved in the general direction of the dune. "On the other side," Lina answered, sand raining from between her fingers. "Managed to kick the engines in at the last second and angle it over the hill so it would land upright. Sorta."

Cabe sighed and sunk to the ground again, relief smeared across his face like fresh tuna.

"Not sure she'll fly properly again without a major overhaul," Lina continued, "but I'm certain she'll be okay." The engineer let out a loud sigh and shrugged. "Mostly. I think. Maybe."

"You think?" Cabe asked.

Lina shrugged. "Hey, what do I know? You're the damn pilot. Nobody ever taught me to land, and you should have remembered that before you went leaping out the cockpit without telling me what you had in mind." She gestured toward the downed craft. "I blame you for that."

Cabe groaned, flopping down beside her, stirring up his own storm of dusty brown in his wake.

Torbon ran his hand over his brow, clearing dirt from his fur, and peered over his shoulder, back in the direction they'd come. "Well, if it's any consolation, the aliens aren't chasing us anymore."

Taj sighed. It very much was a consolation.

It would be a long enough walk back to Culvert City

without being shot at. And despite all her frustration with the boring, mundane existence of her life on Krawlas, her angsty, teenage yearnings for adventure were still alive and well. Taj realized then, if she never got shot at again, she would be fine with that.

Somehow, though, she didn't think that would be the case.

CHAPTER FIVE

"What news have you, Vort?" Grand Admiral Galforin asked through a wavering connection on the view screen in Vort's quarters. The connection was still weak, despite his man's assurance that the transponders were repaired. "Last you reported, you stumbled across that damnable Federation witch, Bethany Anne, and her foul brood."

A dark eyebrow rose, the admiral's orange eyes piercing the captain with something that toed so close to the line of excitement that it took Vort a moment to recognize it. He had never seen anything of the like on the admiral's face before.

"Dare I hope, with you alive and reaching out, that you have rid us of that scum once and for all?" Spittle glistened at the corner of the old Wyyvan admiral's mouth, gleaming across the light years.

Captain Vort stiffened, feet shuffling in place, out of sight of his lord. He remained quiet, disentangling his tongue, knowing full well he'd have to disappoint the grand admiral before he could circle back around to the good news.

For all his bravado as he strolled from the bridge to his cabin, he found himself suddenly questioning whether the news was good enough to satisfy Galforin. Especially after Vort made it clear he'd failed to bring down the empress despite having the drop on her, his ship hidden in the asteroid field.

"Your reticence worries me, Vort," the admiral told him.

It worried Vort, too.

He stared at the grand admiral, taking in the details as he pried at his confidence to shake it loose. Galforin was an imposing figure, his presence commanding, even through the vast distance of space.

Where most Wyyvan were tall and lithe, more gristle and bone than meat, Grand Admiral Galforin was the exception. He stood taller than even the tallest of his subordinates and was easily three to four times as broad.

A mixture of muscle and fat, genetics and scientific alteration, the grand admiral had his command post's doors widened to accommodate his bulk. Two meters across at the shoulder, if not more, his arms were great knots of tension ending at meaty hands, which could easily close about Vort's skull and crush it without effort.

And though the admiral might not be fast when compared to his brethren, if any of the Wyyvan could truly be considered as such, the tree trunks of his legs and battle tank hull of his chest assured Vort there would be no surviving the man's attack should he manage to clasp hold of an opponent.

Many were the stories of Wyyvan recruits being made to clean the gore of Galforin's dissatisfaction from the floor of one command room or another, an abject lesson in not to upset or disappoint the grand admiral were you within arm's reach.

Fortunately for Vort, he and the crew of the Monger were stranded upon Krawlas. The certainty that Galforin wouldn't travel all the way to end of the known universe to personally murder Vort gave the captain the barest ember of courage.

No, instead, I'll die here, abandoned on this godforsaken backwater planet, surrounded by the bones of savages and the dust of my future.

Vort sighed. "Sadly, Admiral, I have no good news as it regards to the Federation's Empress."

"Queen, Vort, not empress," Galforin corrected with a snort. "Let's not raise the pathetic human scum up any higher than her people already have."

The captain stiffened. *Queen, empress? Who can keep track?* "Regardless, Grand Admiral, I must report my failure."

Galforin drew in a slow, deep breath, letting it out moments later under the guise of a rumbling grunt. "I expected no less of you, Vort," he said, eyes narrowing into slits. "Tell me, Captain, how did the Federation wench steal your glory from you?"

"Her craft, the *Archangel II*, is a fortress of steel and death, Admiral."

"And is not the *Monger*?"

"Indeed, but I fear the Federation has evolved since last we crossed ships with them," Vort told the grand admiral, doing his best to wrap his failure in the sweetest of coat-ings. "I unloaded the whole of the *Monger's* guns on her, yet she shrugged our blasts aside as if they were gralflies, Admiral."

"Did she now?"

"She did." Vort swallowed hard, determined to go on. "Our logs will show we caught her unaware, in open space, but not even the combined efforts of our guns could crack her hull, despite having pushed their way through her shields. We left little more than scorch marks upon her side."

Galforin chuckled, a great, rumbling thunder that made Vort's heart gallop in his chest. "How then are you still alive if you were so outmatched, Captain? Did she offer you a deal or show you mercy as she watched you tuck your tail between your legs and flee for your life? Was she so generous as to pat your ass as you ran, Vort?"

The captain stiffened. Now was the moment of truth Vort feared. It was one thing to admit defeat, to tell his admiral that he was beaten in battle. It was quite another to inform the man that a lowly bitch in service to humans had deemed the *Monger*—and by association, Vort—as nothing, a speck of dust to be wiped from her hull and ignored.

"If I'm to be honest, Admiral, I'm not even certain the emp...er, *queen* herself knew her ship had been attacked." Vort bit back a groan at his admission and soldiered on. "The *Archangel II* returned fire, wreaking havoc upon the *Monger* and its engines, sending us listing while...while..."

"While *what*, Vort?"

The captain's chin dipped. "While the ship continued

through the Zendarin Gate as though we didn't exist, Admiral."

Galforin stared for several long seconds, only to burst into raucous laughter. He leaned back in his command seat and roared, his chest and belly dancing beneath the tight confines of his uniform. Tears glistened in the grand admiral's eyes as he went on, dots of spittle flying and peppering the view screen.

Vort suffered the admiral's amusement for several long minutes. There seemed to be no end to the man's laughter. It was only when Vort rose to his full height and cleared his throat that the grand admiral seemed to remember the captain was even there. At last, Galforin reined himself in, though it seemed that nothing would wipe the toothy grin from the wide split of his serpentine lips.

"You couldn't even beat the woman's AI?" Another burst of laughter spilled from the grand admiral, the sound like a dozen worgs barking. "And here I had such high hopes for you when your father came to me, begging me to hand you a command posting, despite your disappointing service record."

He shook his head, the green-gray of his skin blurring against the static backdrop of the view screen. "If nothing else, at least your father's wishful thinking, and his generous donation, of course, served the Wyyvan Empire some good."

"Don't count me out so soon, Admiral," Vort muttered, only realizing at the last moment that the words had actually slithered from his tongue against his best interest of self-preservation.

"What was that, Captain?" The admiral's smile faded

away, and he leaned forward, glaring into the screen as his fists clenched in his lap. "I don't believe I heard you."

"Forgive me, Admiral, but I have yet to tell you of the bounty attached to my unfortunate defeat."

"There's a nugget of brightness in the handfuls of shit you've shoveled my way, Vort? Please, enlighten me as to what might be so valuable as to offset your rank failure as a ship's captain." The admiral leaned back, barely suppressing a chuckle, the grin once more returned to his face.

Captain Vort's fingers played across his console, packaging the file Commander Dard had prepared and streaming it across the cosmos to Wyyvan Command. "If you would look at the document I sent you, Admiral, you'd see that, despite the *Monger*'s inability to drag the bitch to heel, not all is lost. Not remotely."

Galforin's orange gaze shifted to his monitor, and his eyes widened for an instant before he yanked them back in line, hiding his reaction behind a muffled cough. "Interesting," he muttered after a moment. "Are you certain these numbers are correct, Captain?"

"I'd stake my life on them, sir," Vort vowed.

"You do indeed," Galforin agreed, tapping the screen with a long, jagged nail before turning to someone sitting out of sight behind him. "Clear the room. Now!"

A great shuffle sounded in the background, stomping feet followed by the hiss and swish of doors, then the sullen *thump* of them closing on an empty room.

Galforin leaned into the screen. "If these numbers are as true as you say, Vort, you might well have found the one, and only, way to dig yourself free of the vorp pit you've submerged your head into." The admiral sat back and grinned, the points of his mouth stretching all the way to the knotted holes of his ears. "Does anyone else know of this?"

Vort shook his head. "Only my second in command, Admiral, and none others. Not even the residents of this horrid planet, for the Toradium-42 is un-mined, left to rot in the soil, untouched." Vort allowed himself the slightest of grins at the admiral's sudden interest. "Were the empire to provide me with the means to mine the Toradium-42 and transport it back to Belor Prime, the emperor would surely reward you greatly. There has never been such a wealth of Toradium-42 found in one location."

"And the emperor would, no doubt, reward you, as well, would he not?" Galforin asked, not bothering to hide his amusement. "But know your place, Captain. You are my agent, my *servant*, and your success is mine, just as your failure is my shame."

"Of course, Admiral."

"For this," Grand Admiral Galforin tapped the monitor, a loud clicking noise echoing across the galaxies, "and for this alone, I'll forgive you your incompetence. But know this, Vort, should these numbers prove untrue, or should you fail me in this endeavor, there will be no place in our universe, or any other, which will save you or your bloodline from my wrath. Do I make myself clear?"

"Perfectly, Admiral," Vort replied, offering an obsequious nod, hiding the slightest of smiles. Despite the threat to him and his family, this was the best Vort could have hoped for.

"Then we have an understanding." Galforin licked his

lips, his tongue flailing, and grinned into the view screen. "Now, tell me, Captain, what do you need to bring this wellspring home to me?"

Captain Vort told the grand admiral and signed off, reveling in the afterglow of his manipulative success in turning the worst of disasters into a windfall. He sank into his chair and groaned, lazily triggering the comm with a slapping hand.

"Commander Dard?"

"Sir," his second's voice came back to him, sharp and crisp.

"I've changed my mind," he told the man. "Gather the troops and prepare them for battle. We've a city to raze." He chuckled as he silenced the connection. "I don't want a single creature left alive on this planet by nightfall."

"Sir!" Dard called out, cutting the connection to do as he was ordered.

Vort chuckled. If the price of success was as meager as sacrificing the lives of all the local inhabitants of Krawlas, then that was a price Vort was more than happy to pay.

CHAPTER SIX

As it turned out, the *Thorn* wasn't quite as bad off as Taj had expected.

Though, that's not to say it was good.

It managed to limp back to Culvert City, Torbon riding the wing like a balboran rodeo rider, eyes wide and knuckles white to offset the loss of the stabilizer. He squeaked awkwardly every time the engines sputtered or coughed, or when Cabe throttled the overwrought engine.

Taj sat in the harness on the other side, offering up enough counterbalance to keep the windrider from giving in to the broken stabilizer's desire to spin the ship like a top and send them toppling again.

When they finally reached the border of Culvert City, Cabe geared down and landed the craft in the dirt outside of town, whirls of gray and black smoke billowing from the engine.

The streets were brimming with Furlorians, folks desperate to know what happened and to get news regarding the crashed ship. A dozen or more raced to meet the crew, swarming around and hurling questions at them like stones.

"What is it?"

"Where did it come from?"

"What do they look like?"

"Why are they here?"

"Are they dangerous?"

Taj raised a hand to silence the crowd, but the arrival of Gran Beaux, his cane tapping a rhythmic warning on the packed dirt street, was what really settled the throng.

They moved aside to let him pass as he hobbled up from behind, slow and steady and steely-eyed. His gray fur stood out sharp around his pink nose, which looked as if it had been cut in half longwise and stitched back poorly. Between that and the constant glower etched into his brow, he always looked ready to take a kitten to task, despite his generally calm demeanor.

He ambled forward, not saying a word until he was right on top of the crew, much to the chagrin of the impatient crowd. They wanted answers, and they wanted them now, but Gran Beaux never rushed anything. No power on Krawlas would ever change that.

So, they shuffled in place, muttering under their breaths, knowing their complaints were useless, until the thin Tom came to a halt and drew a slow, deep breath. He leaned hard against his cane, and his ribs twitched beneath his thin, pale fur.

"Soooo…?" he asked.

"We're in trouble, Gran," Taj told him, the rest of the crew clearly happy to let her take the lead. She was Gran

Beaux's favorite, after all. "Aliens have crashed, and they're not friendly."

"That's an understatement," Torbon muttered.

Beaux gave him a sideways glance before turning his focus back to Taj. "What makes you think that, girl?"

"They gacking shot at us, that's why!" Torbon shouted, realizing at the last moment that he said it aloud. He covered his mouth as Gran snarled, eyes narrowed into tiny amber slits. "Stomped out of their ship and let loose," Torbon continued, mumbling through his paw as if he couldn't stop himself.

"They did what?"

Taj nodded. "They shot at us, Gran. Tore the *Thorn* up good, and nearly us, too." She showed him her torn sleeve and the wreckage of her uniform. The stains of her blood had faded a little but were still obvious, and the wound was red and raw.

Gran Beaux was a soldier, born and bred, despite his advanced years. He turned to a nearby Tom, waving a gnarled paw. "Run and gather the elders and tell them to call a gatherin'. And we need a posse formed up right away, in case we need to head out and make a point."

Taj shook her head, grabbing the Tom by the arm to keep him from bolting off right away. "With respect, Gran, these aren't some ragtag group of mercenaries we can fend off with old bolt pistols and hunting rifles. They're organized, armored, armed, and deadly. Soldiers, an army of some kind. If we go out there again, even if it's just to show a presence to try and make a point, a lot of our people are gonna get killed."

"They came in a destroyer, Gran," Lina added, shuffling

up alongside Taj, using her as a buffer between her and Beaux. "A *real* destroyer, not some fluffed-up pleasure ship."

"A destroyer?" Beaux's eyes narrowed even further, his nose scrunched into a tiny knot of fluttering whiskers.

The fact that he didn't ask Lina for confirmation about the alien ship's classification made it clear he took what they said seriously, and Taj loved him for it.

He scratched at his chin, short, ragged claws *scritching* against rough, patchy fur that had long since passed white. "Seems you kids are right. Might be best if we find some-place to hunker down first, see what they want before we make contact. No one who fires on children without warning or cause is no one we want to hold a friendly hand out to, anyway."

Most of the group nodded in agreement, heads bobbing, Torbon most of all, though, for once, he actually kept his mouth shut.

Taj let the Tom loose after Beaux's declaration, and he darted off to pass along Gran's message, but she couldn't help but shudder at the thought of what they would have to do soon. She couldn't picture these aliens doing anything but what they'd already done: shoot at peaceful Furlorians. The next time, people wouldn't be so lucky to escape with a few cuts and scrapes. Of that, she was certain.

While Culvert city was the primary settlement on Krawlas, the largest of the three established, it was little more than an outpost on the far edge of the Omaratus Universe. The Furlorians settled there because of its out-of-the-way location, its distance from other "civilized" worlds.

Those Furlorians who'd wanted even less to do with others after the horrors of the war spread across the planet to live or die on their own, having little to no contact with those of Culvert City.

Gran Beaux and the other survivors hadn't wanted anything more to do with modern civilization after their escape, and for good reason, or so it seemed to Taj today. And while that had kept Krawlas peaceful, a good place to raise self-reliant litters without the stresses of a fast-paced or corrupt society, it had stripped the Furlorians of the one thing they'd had in abundance on their old world: technology.

These days, the most viable tech they had was the *Thorn*, a windrider crafted from the spare parts of a broken-down, sub-orbital fighter and a crop duster, as well as the *Paradigm* and the *Voltar*. The latter had been the two antiquated freighters the people had traveled to Krawlas in. The *Paradigm* was the only one that remained functional. The *Voltar* had been scavenged for parts over the ages.

Neither of the ships had been considered high tech, not even the day after they'd been built. They'd been created more for grunt duty and hauling supplies and people than anything resembling warfare. And while the sturdy freighters had seen the Furlorians through the harshness of space after the war, that journey and the intervening years of minimal maintenance and over-use hadn't done the last remaining ship any favors.

Much like the *Thorn* and Gran Beaux, the *Paradigm* was

a temperamental old beast, getting by more on stubbornness rather than any real upkeep. It had run out of any substantive fuel source cycles ago and had been hidden away inside an underground cavern to keep it from being picked up by orbital scans.

Rowl only knew if the ship still functioned on more than an essential level. If the Furlorians had to rely on the freighter to see them free of their current predicament, as they had so long ago, Taj knew they were spitting into a sparkstorm.

"We are so screwed," Torbon muttered. Lina elbowed him in the ribs before Taj could do it. He grunted, covering his side against another attack. "What? I'm only saying what we're all thinking."

"Keep it to yourself, boy," Beaux told him. "Now ain't the time for defeatist thinking, ya hear? We got more important things to focus on."

"Yes, sir." Torbon dropped his chin to his chest, offering a shallow nod of deference.

Taj didn't believe he meant it for an instant, but it sure didn't hurt to show some respect to Gran Beaux. Otherwise the smack he got from Lina would be nothing compared to catching a blow across the head from Gran's cane. Wouldn't have been the first time it happened.

"'Sides, we don't even know what these folks want yet. All this could be a misunderstanding, their folks spooked by you popping up out of nowhere. No telling how disoriented these aliens might be after their crash."

Taj stared at the old Tom, peering into the slits of his eyes. She knew him too well to think he actually believed that, but she didn't question him out loud since it was clear he was playing to the crowd and managing expectations.

It was how he oversaw the settlement since they'd arrived, and long before. It was a skill he'd done his best to pass on to Taj over the turns, grooming her to take over in his stead when the fateful—and, hopefully, far off—day came that he could no longer do it himself.

She wasn't looking forward to being in charge. Fortunately, she didn't have to be today.

Beaux waved the crowd away. "Go home, get your families, and head on over to the meeting hall so we can figure out what needs to be done. And don't dawdle. Don't know what kind of time we're looking at 'fore these aliens come a calling. Best to be prepared and waiting than caught with our tails stuck between our cheeks."

The throng started off, muttering and whispering among themselves, casting furtive glances back toward Gran Beaux and the crew, as if hoping to overhear something more before they moved on too far. Beaux, though, held his tongue until they were all well out of earshot, shooing them on with a wave of his cane every time they slowed even a tiny bit. Then he turned back and met the eyes of each of the crew, one after another, until he settled on Taj.

"Don't no one come here on purpose," he started, "or for good reason."

"Besides us?" Torbon asked.

Cabe sighed, and Beaux shuffled in place, propped against his cane.

"That's why we're out here, boy, to stay as far away from other folks as possible. No good comes of being overly neighborly to an advanced species, I tell ya. Know this from experience, I do, having tried to settle a few other places before we found this here planet. That these folks came in shooting first, not bothering to ask questions, tells me I'm right. We're looking at a rough few days unless we can scatter to the wind or find a good place to hunker down, out of sight, out of mind."

"So, we hide?" Cabe asked. "Is that what we're supposed to do?"

Beaux shuffled forward and clasped a hand on Cabe's shoulder, squeezing. "I know I done been teaching you to fight and fly your whole gacking life, boy, but that's for when your scruff's against the wall and ain't no other way. No point in risking our necks if we can scamper for a dark hole and stay outta sight until the situation becomes clearer, safer. Fighting's a last resort. If no one gets hurt, that's the way I'd prefer to go, ya hear?"

Cabe nodded. Taj knew he didn't quite agree, the excitement of doing something, anything, other than chasing loose balborans or herding trrilacs were what the crew dreamed of. Excitement was sparse on Krawlas, worse so in Culvert City, the *pinnacle* of modernity here at the edge of the universe. Still, Taj could tell Cabe understood where old Gran was coming from despite his reservations.

Quiet and peaceful, boring as it might be, it was safe. Everyone went home for dinner at night and woke up healthy, barring old age or the rare accident. The arrival of a destroyer packed tight with trigger-happy soldiers stuck on the planet, while interesting and new for sure, was a threat to the Furlorians existence. One that could bring death and destruction to everyone they knew. They couldn't take their arrival lightly.

Beaux shook Cabe's shoulder. "Now, go on and get to the hall, all of ya," he said, "but before ya do, be sure to swing by the armory and let old Rogue there know I told him to set you up with some firepower. Nothing fancy, ya hear, but some good, solid pistols or two. Maybe a rifle, in case our alien friends get to showing up early." He tugged Cabe forward, inching out of the way to let him pass. "And hurry. I'll meet you in the hall shortly."

Taj grunted her acknowledgement and pushed Torbon and Lina forward, forcing them to move along with Cabe. "Will do, Gran. Be careful, whatever you plan on doing," she told him, knowing he had something in mind. It wouldn't be Beaux if he didn't.

He grinned and shooed them off. "Don't ya be worrying about me, girl. Take care of business like I said, and I'll see ya soon."

Taj nodded and started off, but let her gaze linger over her shoulder on the old Tom. As much as he'd been a stable presence in her life, ever since she could recall peeling her eyes open the first time, she couldn't help but think this might well be the last time she ever saw him.

An empty pit opened in her stomach at the thought, and she felt flush, not looking away until he disappeared from sight as the crew marched down the street.

Never before in her life had she wanted to be more wrong than right then.

CHAPTER SEVEN

Gran Merr, or Mama as everyone called her instead of using her official title, stood at the podium, unconsciously clacking her claws against the wood in a steady rhythm, whiskers flittering.

Unlike Beaux, who had a rugged brusqueness to him, despite his thinning fur and aging frame, Mama was a wisp of a woman who always bore a smile for everyone; at least to their face.

She had sharp claws when she needed them, as Taj could attest, having seen them up close more than a time or two growing up wild like she had after her mom had passed on.

Mama's fur had long ago turned white, like snow on a high mountain peak, reflecting the light of the hall with brilliant sparkles. She had on spectacles that magnified the emerald of her eyes, and there was no mistaking the intelligence lurking behind the glasses. She stared out over the crowd, waiting quietly as the group debated back and forth about her last statement.

The gathering was torn between riding out to meet the aliens and hiding away in the narrow catacombs that ran beneath Culvert City. It was one of the more functional reasons the Grans had decided to settle where they had on Krawlas. While the tunnels were little more than a labyrinthine mass of crawlspaces, somewhat re-shaped for better function, they had saved the Furlorians from a number of past tragedies, from trrilac stampedes to tornados.

Unfortunately for those here now, the population of Culvert City had grown beyond those early days. While still barely numbering two hundred or so Furlorians in the wayward town, that was probably eighty more than could comfortably squeeze into the warrens while still giving them room to move and store supplies. That left a lot of folks scrambling for someplace to hide if things went south with the aliens.

A cold chill crept spider-like down Taj's spine at the thought of what might happen if things turned violent. Furlorians were good at scattering, darting into the wilderness to vanish.

A good number of their people had gone nomad cycles back, but Taj knew there'd be nowhere to hide on the barren planet if the aliens turned the full might of their efforts to finding them.

The warrens were safe, for a time. The thick rock and minerals of the planet deflected deep scans, but the rest of the world was open fields and broad spaces. There was nothing providing long-term shelter or cover from the elements or encroaching forces.

All it would take was for a few of the Furlorians trapped outside to be captured before a dedicated alien menace learned the location of the rest of the people. As brave, strong, and independent as Furlorians were, they'd been alone on Krawlas for gack-near a century now. Only the Grans were true warriors, the only ones among them who had seen non-simulated combat. Taj couldn't picture them holding their own, or their tongue, for long under duress.

"As I was saying..." Mama Merr's voice broke through the clamor, subtly reminding folks that her presence was as sharp as her claws. The crowd grew quiet in a rush. "We're not being given much in the way of options here. I know several of you want to gather arms and rush out to meet these aliens, confront them and see what they want before they come to us, which is inevitable given that they crashed here and are likely stuck. Still, what do we know of these aliens?"

"They love their guns!" Torbon called out, hiding his face and muffling his voice to try and keep from being recognized.

Mama Merr nodded, pointing a finger in the general direction of the crew, who lingered near the back. "Torbon is right," she said, calling him out despite his pathetic attempt at subterfuge.

Cabe and Lina chuckled, and Taj muzzled her own laugh as Torbon's cheeks burned red beneath his fur. His Aunt Jadie shook her head at him from across the room, shushing him with a paw to her lips.

Mama went on. "They opened fire on our children, offering nothing but violence from the get-go."

"That's why we need to hit 'em back!" Grady called out from the front row, his flabby, striped-cheeks wiggling beneath the weight of his thick whiskers. "We need to show these aliens they can't come here and roust us out of our homes 'cause their bad luck landed 'em here on *our* home." A mutter of agreement floated through the crowd. "We done staked our claim to Krawlas, and ain't no one got the right to take that from us. We earned our place, and I'll be gacked if some stranded aliens are gonna take it from us." More folks raised their voices in support, the room erupting into heated debate once more.

"Too true," Mama called out, slicing through the noise like she was scraping mud, shaking it from her claws. "But when's the last time you used your rifle for something other than scooching your nip pouch across the porch because you were too lazy to get up out your chair and grab it, Grady? Have you even cleaned that thing since we landed here? Got any energy packs with juice left?"

Muffled laughter burst to life, stilling only when Grady stiffened in his seat and turned to stare at the crowd. The amusement flickered back to life the moment he turned back around to glare at Gran.

"The same goes for the rest of you before you start in on Grady as if he's the only one," Mama told them, gesturing toward the gathered throng, shaking a finger at each. "None of us have had to battle for our lives since we set down here, so long ago. Yeah, maybe we've had some trials and tribulations, hard and lean times now and again, but no one's pointed a weapon at your head and tried to punch a hole in it to take what's yours."

She straightened as best as her back would allow and let her green gaze roam the assembly. "I don't see but maybe thirty old-timers in all the faces here, veterans who've seen action, who have spilled blood in the name of our people, and most of them are near as old as me and Gran Beaux."

"Ain't nobody that old!" someone shouted.

The laughter reared to life again as Mama's smile broadened before fading a degree or two a moment later. "That may be true, but I've held the futures of living beings in my hands before, felt the warmth of someone's life dripping wet and sticky between my claws. How many of you can say that?"

There were a few muffled acknowledgments, the oldest of the Furlorians muttering that they had, faces hard with shame, grief, or some emotion Taj wasn't entirely sure she understood or recognized.

Regardless, those grizzled few certainly didn't look as if they relished getting into another fight or having that thrust upon them again. It was the younger ones who looked angry, determined, ready to go to war.

She recognized the gleam in their eyes as she turned and glanced at her crew. They, too, had the same shimmer, a coloring in their cheeks that highlighted their excitement. Yes, they were obviously worried, scared even, but she could see they wanted to stand up for something, to fight to defend their home like the stories the old Grans had told them.

They clearly understood there would be a cost, but since none of them had paid such a price before, including

Taj, she was certain they were oblivious to what was to come. She sure was, though her imagination more than filled in the horrible gaps.

Taj fiddled with the bolt pistol strapped to her leg, an errand claw running its length. It was one thing to imagine fighting for your life, getting drawn into the romanticism of protecting one's home and kin like they told of in the books and holos, but the reality of it was etched across the faces of the Grans and elders.

There was reluctance there and, to Taj's surprise, real fear, something she couldn't recall having ever seen before. She stared at the crew's faces for several long, silent moments, wondering what was running through their minds. And then it struck her, a hazy memory of a conversation she'd had with Gran Beaux long before she even reported for her first day of service. She'd been little more than a kitten.

The elders didn't want to avoid war because they were scared of dying, but because they were afraid of what it would do to those made to serve, how it would impact their lives and futures. Their own lives had been made harder, more bitter, darker—jaded Beaux had once said.

Taj remembered hearing the Grans lament the loss of innocence that had happened in the aftermath, and how the young paid the price for it all. Beaux and Mama didn't want that for their litters, and that's why they'd settled so far from the rest of the populated universe, hoping to escape such cruelty by avoiding the cause of it. Other people.

Still, as fate would have it, no one escaped the bleaker aspects of life for long, no matter how hard they tried.

Taj sighed and pulled her gaze from the ground and placed it back on Mama Merr as the old Gran went on.

"I don't want any more blood on my hands, and I know none of the other Grans do either. As such, I think it best that we—"

A massive explosion cut her off, the whole room shuddering under their feet. Whirls of dust stirred in the rafters, and the boards creaked. A harsh whistle screeched nearby, and there was another explosion, another shaking the ground. The front doors of the meeting hall were flung open.

"The aliens are here already! Shuttles brought them," an older Tom shouted through cupped hands as he stepped through the doorway. He looked flustered, winded.

"How many?" Taj asked, but her question would never be answered.

Painfully familiar green bolts of energy tore through the door frame, and the old Tom's back at the same time. Wood splintered and went flying, followed by blood and shards of bone.

The old Tom grunted as he was knocked forward by the impact of multiple blaster shots. Black holes welled at his chest before his shirt ran red. Wide-eyed, his voice stolen along with his life, he crumpled to the floor without a sound. The assemblage stared on, frozen in place until Mama Merr's voice cut the strings of their hesitance.

"To the tunnels! Now," she shrieked, dragging the last syllables out into a growl.

More bolts tore through the door as if to emphasize her order. Taj grabbed Cabe and pushed him into the aisle between the seats. "We need to cover their escape," she shouted, whipping her bolt pistol free of its holster.

Cabe followed suit, and Lina and Torbon crowded behind them as the throng bolted for the tunnel entrance hidden at the base of the dais Mama stood upon.

Taj dared a glance in Mama's direction and saw the Gran next to the secret entrance of the tunnels, already opened. She waved her arms, calling for the nearest Furlorians to clamber inside. Her smile was a grimace now, her light fur even paler as she ushered her people into hiding. More blasts tore the wall at the front of the hall open, forcing Taj's attention back to the alien threat outside.

"They're not gonna make it," Taj and Lina said in unison, sharing the uncomfortable thought. The two darted forward, Cabe right alongside. Torbon trailed a meter or so behind, fumbling with his weapon, which was still in its holster.

"I'm not liking this hero gack," he muttered.

Mama Merr continued to shout in the background as the gathered Furlorians ran for cover. The older ones, alongside the Grans, formed up and shouted right along, hurrying the rest toward safety. A few raised their weapons, but the crowd muddled their aim.

Right then, three of the armored aliens stormed the shattered front entryway, blasters leveled, firing without hesitation. Several lagging Furlorians were shot in the back as they scrambled to hide. The smell of charred fur and blood filled the room as they collapsed.

"Gacking Rowl!" Taj screamed.

Her hand trembled, knuckles aching as she clasped the bolt pistol's grip so hard she was afraid she'd drop it. She'd never before shot at another living being with her weapon, knowing the consequences were irreversible. Once you killed someone, there was no taking it back.

Dead was dead, and as much as she craved the excitement of a real battle, she'd never once given much thought to the idea that she'd have to actually end someone's life in order to protect herself or her friends and family. Now that the situation stood before her, black armor and searing green bolts of energy flying every which way, the moment of truth was upon her.

She cast a furtive glance to the bodies curled up on the floor, oozing blood and staring without ever seeing again. Another Furlorian fell, the back of his head blasted open, joining the ranks of the dead on the ground.

That was when Taj realized she couldn't worry about her innocence, couldn't worry about what the fight would do to her conscience, her soul. She only knew she had to save lives.

That in mind, she squeezed the trigger, and the bolt pistol *thumped* in her hand. Unlike the blasters the aliens carried, quietly hissing as it released its energy in smooth, economical bursts, Taj's primitive pistol barked, firing a marble-sized wad of barely contained energy. It struck the nearest alien in the chest and exploded, tearing open the alien's armor and the flesh inside. The soldier shrieked and stumbled backward, out of the building, a smoking crater where his chest used to be.

Taj couldn't help but grin at the results. While her bolt pistol was an antique as far as these aliens were concerned, it packed a far greater punch than most weapons, acting more like a grenade launcher than a pistol.

TIM MARQUITZ

The other aliens paused at seeing their companion blasted away by the strange weapon. They turned their weapons from the fleeing Furlorians to those standing before them, realizing where the true threat lay.

"You little fuzz-headed rodent," one of the soldiers screamed, and Taj was caught off guard by his vehemence, realizing she could understand the alien. She only then remembered that Beaux had insisted that all her people inject the tiny translators beneath their temples as part of their service to Krawlas, to better prepare them should anyone ever stumble across their out of the way home.

It was also only then that she registered what the alien had called her.

She stiffened and glared. "Wait! What did you call me, you slimy lizard?"

Cabe didn't give him the opportunity to respond. A bolt from his pistol slammed into the alien's visor, nearly blowing the creature's head clean off.

Wisps of smoke rose from the soldier's cracked helmet as if it were a volcano erupting. Steam hissed out a moment later, and the alien keeled over. Lina and Torbon fired at the last of the aliens as the other fell, blasting two holes in his chest and sending him flying out to join the first of the dead aliens.

"Did you see that?" Torbon shouted. A giant grin showed his eyeteeth gleaming in the light of the meeting hall.

"Don't celebrate yet," Taj told him, recovering her composure. The sound of blaster fire continued outside. "There are more than these three out there. Let's get to the door and surveil."

70

The crew started forward only to hear another whistle sound somewhere nearby. Taj stiffened.

"Incoming!" Lina shouted, ducking on instinct, hours and hours of holo training films clearly having sunk in.

Taj recognized the sound from earlier and fought the urge to follow suit, but she knew she needed to do more than cower. She cast a quick glance over her shoulder at Mama Merr and the fleeing townspeople.

While a good number of her people had managed to slip inside the tunnel entrance and disappear, there were far too many still lingering near Mama and the entry. She knew they wouldn't all fit, but they needed to get as many of them as they could before the rest of the aliens arrived at the hall and figured out where they'd gone, seeing the hatch open and voiding their effort.

An explosion rocked the roof of the hall and blasted a hole in it. Wood and shrapnel rained downed over the congregation. Mama Merr howled as debris peppered her. She ducked low, sheltering those slipping into the tunnels, but there was too much wreckage.

She folded beneath the weight of it, a wooden beam breaking loose of the roof and striking her low on the back. Her hiss of pain was buried under the crash of the beam's impact.

"*Nooooo!*" Taj spun around and bounded toward Mama, screaming.

She scrambled over the rubble of the roof, slipping and clawing her way up the dais to Mama's side. By the time she reached her, the remaining Furlorians had pulled the beam free of her legs, but Mama lay there, eyes wide and glassy with obvious agony. She trembled, and Taj slid to the ground beside her, pushing past the others and pulling Mama into her arms.

"Mama?" Taj whispered, barely able to get the word out. Dust choked her throat.

Hand shaking, Mama Merr reached up with a weak hand and grabbed Taj's ear, tugging at it. "Ge-get them...t-to...safety. The-there's—"

"No," Taj growled. "I'm not leaving you."

The crew staggered to her side, and Taj glanced to the tunnel entrance, seeing the worried faces staring up at her through the cloud of dust. More explosions boomed outside, and Taj could hear the stomp of heavy boots through the ringing in her ears as soldiers marched toward the hall. She knew there wasn't much time before the aliens were on them in force.

"Help me get her into the hole." Taj gestured for Cabe and Torbon to help.

Cabe stepped past Taj and scooped Mama Merr up while Torbon dropped into the tunnel entrance, scattering those watching from below.

"Pass her down," Torbon called out.

Lina helped Cabe guide the Gran into the waiting arms of Torbon. Mama shook her head, but that was the extent of her defiance, too weak to do anything else but glare. Taj groaned at seeing her so weak, so frail looking. Covered in a thin layer of dust, Mama was ghostly, and only the narrow flutter of her emerald eyes, and the puff of dust as she breathed, made it clear she was still alive.

As Torbon carried Mama deeper into the tunnel to situate her someplace safe, Taj returned her attention to the door only to see black shapes swarming outside. "Gack! They're coming. Everyone, out back. Scatter to the desert!"

Taj hopped to her feet and fired her bolt pistol through the hall's doorway, hoping to delay the aliens long enough for the remaining townsfolk to flee and to hide the entrance to the tunnel. The Furlorians fled, racing for the back door, while Lina and Cabe spun about to join her in shooting at the aliens.

Taj growled under her breath. "Keep Mama safe," she told them, reaching out and grabbing Cabe by his scruff. She yanked hard, dumping him in the hole without warning. He squeaked and tumbled away, thumping against the floor in the tunnel below.

Lina's head snapped to the side as Cabe disappeared, and Taj popped off a few more shots at the door, then grabbed her.

"Wait. I'll—"

Taj didn't give her time to finish. Lina let out a quick chitter as Taj yanked her back and deposited her in the tunnel with the others. Lina hissed at her as she fell.

"I'll be right behind you," Taj said and went to seal the hatch to the tunnels.

That's when a black-clad arm appeared in the front doorway, snapping around the corner. Something flew from the alien's hand, and it took a moment for Taj to process what she saw. Metal gleamed off the silver device, small and round, almost like a ball, and her heart galloped in her chest, banging against her ribs.

"Get down!" she screamed and slammed the hatch closed. She turned away, covering her head and burying it in the debris piled atop the dais. The device clattered down the aisle somewhere behind her. Then it exploded.

A wave of heat flared past her, curling her fur, and then she was struck by what felt like a million furious sticker burs lashing at her back, throwing her forward into the wreckage.

A few seconds after that, she was lucky not to feel anything.

CHAPTER EIGHT

The world spun as Taj came to. A sharp keening set her ears and whiskers to twitching. It was as if her skull had exploded right alongside the grenade. She gasped, drawing a fetid breath and choking on dust, then rolled to her back with a grunt. Every bone in her body ached, and it was like prying a mountain loose from the ground to open her eyes.

When she finally managed the herculean task, she regretted it instantly.

Hovering above her, their dark shapes wavering, a handful of alien soldiers held their blaster rifles aimed at her, gaping black holes ready to spew death poised inches from her face.

"Oh...gack," she muttered.

She met the oblong, ebony eyeholes glaring at her, and she shifted uncomfortably on the ground. Copper coated her tongue, invading her throat, and she could feel blood running down her nose and across her lips. She blinked away the grit in hopes of clearing her vision, but then wondered why she even bothered. She was about to die.

Did she really want to see it coming?

She hissed at the aliens and heard one chuckle in response, the sound distorted by the faceplate it wore, steam bubbling in the hoses. Puffs of moist air vented from slits where she imagined its mouth would sit.

A moment later, the visor lightened, giving Taj a clear view of the aliens that resides within the armor. Serpent-like, much like the large lizards that roamed the nearby desert, she could see the grins on their wide mouths.

"Are these little things what the captain is so worried about?" one asked, his voice reminding her a little of Lina's garbled communications in the *Thorn*. "Hardly seems worth the effort," he said, not bothering to hide his disgust.

Another shrugged. "Doesn't want the insects getting in the way, is all."

"Let's get this over with," a third said, leaning in, his weapon inching closer.

"What are you worried about? Afraid the little thing's going to bite you." He poked Taj with the barrel of his rifle, the metal *clinking* against her eyetooth. She hissed and pulled back, only causing the soldier to laugh again. "Hardly a galactic terror we're facing here."

He leaned in, with what Taj could only imagine was a grin behind his mask. "It's got claws and teeth, but they aren't anything like what those Federation fangers have going for them. I doubt this one here can even break skin if we let her."

The rest of the aliens laughed along with the first, and Taj felt her cheeks warm. *I'll show them how hard I can bite,* she thought, twitching her tail in the dust, coiling it beneath her to give her a bit of extra leverage.

They'd shot at her and her friends, they'd killed her people, and they'd hurt Mama. Even with as dizzy as she was, her head still swimming, she was going to make them pay for what they'd done.

She pulled back a paw, easing her claws out, clenched her teeth, and made to throw herself at the chuckling alien.

Before she even got off the ground, the soldier's head exploded in a misty cloud of black and green that rained down over her. She gasped, then snapped her mouth shut to keep from inhaling the ruin of the alien's brain and skull.

"Get down, girl!"

Taj recognized Gran Beaux's voice and reacted without hesitation. She ducked low, getting her feet under her while she did, and cast a sideways glance at her rescuer.

He stormed into the room like a hero from the old holos. He held a bolt pistol in each hand in place of his cane, the guns so old they barely looked real, and squeezed the triggers with abandon. Balls of crackling energy spewed from the barrels with ill-intent. And with the soldiers crowded around each other, there was no place for them to run.

They lifted their rifles in reply, but it was far too late. Bolts of energy slammed into the aliens, ripping open their armor and scorching the flesh beneath. The soldiers howled and wailed as they were shredded, collapsing into a squirming heap of dead and dying bodies right in front of Taj.

Part of her wanted to laugh, to revel in the well-earned

deaths of the aliens, but that part was fleeting. She choked her mirth back as reality set in. These soldiers before her, however cruel and wicked, were living creatures. Or they were.

They likely had families, people who cared for them, people who depended on them. And now, they were little more than bloody stains on the dirty floor of the ruined meeting hall. They were dead and never coming back, and that struck Taj far worse than she could have imagined.

She swallowed the growing knot in her throat and clambered to her feet as the last of the aliens exhaled its final breath, steam hissing, setting the growing pool of blood on the floor to wavering.

Gran Beaux holstered one of his pistols and rushed as fast as he was able to her side. He looked her over for injuries, grabbing her shoulder and turning her a bit for a better look. She knew she looked battered and bruised, but she'd avoided the majority of the explosion.

"You okay, girl?"

Taj nodded, not trusting her voice yet. A shiver ran spider-like down her spine, setting her fur standing on edge. She gulped in a deep breath of air, doing her best to ignore the coppery stink invading her nose. Her whiskers twitched.

Beaux seemed to understand and didn't push her. "We need to get you out of here. We—"

"Mama Merr's hurt," she mumbled, almost afraid to speak the words, as if putting voice to them would make things worse.

Beaux stiffened. His eyes shifted to where the hatch to the tunnels lay hidden. "Bad?"

Taj nodded. "The roof fell on her. I think her back is bro—" The word crowded her throat, unwilling to let others pass.

Gran Beaux put a hand on her shoulder, giving it a gentle squeeze. "Merr's tough," he told her. "She'll make it."

Taj saw a glimmer of moisture gleaming in Beaux's eyes, and she realized that right that moment was the very first time he'd ever lied to her. The truth was written in the wrinkled lines of his face, the ears flattened to the sides of his head. He looked as ready to burst into tears as Taj felt.

He and Mama had been together since they were kittens. They'd weathered the storm of war on Felinus 4, surviving for years under the harsh rule of the invaders, and had traveled the universe together in search of their new home on Krawlas.

The pair had had countless litters together, and they could account for a third of the bloodlines running through the veins of Taj and the other Furlorians in Culvert City and beyond.

Taj could see every moment of that life being re-lived by Beaux as he stared at Taj, battling his emotions less effectively than he'd handled the alien soldiers shattered around her. She watched him swallow hard, his throat bobbling as he sucked in breath to speak again.

"She'll make it," he repeated. "She has to." The last bit was spoken low, mostly to himself and barely a whisper, but Taj heard the grief in his tone, each word dripping with his feelings for Mama Merr. Taj understood. She felt the same way.

"Yeah, she will," Taj agreed with him, offering as much

support as she could muster, eking a grim smile to color her lips.

Beaux nodded, seeming to rein in his emotions. "Well, we best get out of here before more of them show up. There's a bunch of them bastards still outside." He gestured toward the hatch with his gray chin. "Get that flap open, and let's get ourselves down there quick-like."

Taj couldn't agree more. She spun around and skittered over to the hatch, digging at the edge with her claws to peel it open. A moment later, she sighed as the heavy steel door swung free. The gaping blackness below greeted her.

"All right, Gran, let's—" She was cut short by the sudden burst of rifle fire.

Taj turned to see Beaux struck in the shoulder. He gasped and was whipped about, falling to his knees and scrambling to return fire. Black shapes crowded the doorway, a number of rifle barrels gleaming.

"Beaux!" Taj screamed, diving toward him.

Another shot struck him in the stomach, and he groaned and fell onto his back. His bolt pistols flew loose of his hands and vanished in the piles of debris. She grabbed at him, ready to drag him to the hatch, but another bolt clipped his leg, and he screamed, curling in on himself.

Spittle gleamed at his lips, whiskers pinned to his cheeks, as Taj pawed, trying to get a good grip on him. That's when two of the silver grenades were lobbed into the room, bouncing crazily across the floor and coming to rest nearby. Both Taj and Beaux froze and stared at the devices with wide eyes.

"Come on, Gran, we need to—"

Beaux didn't let her finish. His strength was surprising, considering his wounds, as he grabbed Taj's wrist and peeled her hand loose of him. His other hand, scorched shoulder and all, reached out and pulled at her ankle. Taj froze, wondering what he was doing, and then it became clear.

"Nooooooo!" she screamed, her throat chafing at her ferocity, but there was nothing she could do to stop the old Gran from doing to her what she'd done to her crew.

Her leg pulled out from beneath her, her balance stolen, Taj toppled backward toward the open hatch. She howled as gravity yanked her downward and through the gaping mouth of the tunnel entrance. Wind whipped past her as she fell, and she hit the ground hard, the breath knocked from her lungs.

She gasped, staring upward, trying to gather her wits. A flicker of movement drew her focus, and Beaux's wizened face blocked her view of the hole in the meeting hall's roof. In the crook of his wounded arm, he held the two grenades tucked tight against his chest.

"You take care of Merr for me, Taj, and all the others, too," he told her, meeting her eyes. This time, there was no hiding the tears there—in hers or his. "I'm counting on you to lead them now, to see them all through this, you hear? There's no one else I trust to do this, ya hear?"

"No," she shouted back. "Don't do this! Please!"

He shook his head. "Too late for me," he said. "Live well, darlin'. I'm proud of you."

Taj shuddered, suddenly cold, as Beaux reached out with his other arm and yanked the heavy hatch closed. There was an ominous metallic *thump* as it seated, some shuffling over top, and then Taj was cast in absolute blackness before her eyes could adjust.

Then there was a tremendous *boom* above.

Dirt and pieces of stone peppered Taj, and she scrambled for cover, deeper into the tunnel as the ground trembled. She stumbled and slammed into the rough-hewn wall, and stars erupted before her eyes. Her sight blurred an instant later by fountains of tears. She folded to the ground, sobbing, clawing at the rock to keep from being swept away by her emotions.

A moment later, the earth stopped rumbling, and Taj slid across the wall and flopped onto her back. Silence washed over the tunnel, and the darkness closed on her once again.

The only sound to be heard was Taj's weeping.

CHAPTER NINE

Captain Vort stood before the wreckage of a building, watching black smoke smolder from within the ruins. His soldiers were scattered about the street, heads on a swivel. They looked anywhere except at the bodies of their companions who laid dead in the dirt with holes blasted in them.

Vort went over to the first of the corpses and rolled it over with a callous boot. The soldier's head had nearly been decapitated by a well-placed blast from some form of primitive energy weapon. The wound bore none of the grace of modern weaponry.

He sighed. "Anyone care to explain why these little savages managed to kill so many of you?" Commander Dard stiffened and made ready to respond, as expected, but Vort waved him to silence. "It's not you I want to hear from, Commander. I want to hear it from *them.*"

A nearby soldier inched forward. "They, uh, caught us

off guard, Captain. We believed they would not be prepared for us. Not so soon after our arrival."

"No," Vort replied, shaking his head. "You only opened fire on a group of them the moment the doors to the *Monger* opened. Why wouldn't they be prepared for hostility? Why wouldn't we be?"

"Sir, if I can explain—"

The captain yanked Commander Dard's blaster from his holster and aimed, pulling the trigger. The blast tore through the soldier's visor, turning the metal molten red before it punched through and sprayed what was left of the man's head across the dirt behind him. His body crumpled to the ground right after, landing with a sullen *thump*.

"Anyone else care to explain anything to me?" Vort asked. When no one responded, he drew in a deep breath and let his gaze wander across the gathered soldiers. "I didn't think so."

He handed the pistol back to Dard and circled around the ruined building, where his men had encountered the majority of the furry aliens. He'd expected to see masses of charred bodies, scattered about the streets and walks. Instead, what he saw was disappointment.

While his men had gone out of their way to lay waste to the tiny village, the evidence of that laying in the buildings that smoldered all over, there were hardly any corpses to claim anything resembling success in the matter. He snatched up one of the dead Furlorians by its scruff and stared at its burnt features. Its wide eyes stared back at him, sightless.

"These are what caught you so off guard?" he asked, casting a sour glance over his shoulder at the remaining soldiers who'd elected to stay back, giving him space. No one replied, and Vort grunted, tossing the alien corpse aside. "Somewhere in this cluster of failure, I'm expecting to hear good news." He turned, the steamed air in his hoses bubbling, and raised his arms in expectation. "Anyone?"

Commander Dard stepped forward, tapping the side of his helmet. Though Vort couldn't see his face behind his darkened visor, he could almost sense the man's relieved smile. "There is word, Captain."

"Please, share it with me before I'm forced to borrow your pistol again and create my own good news, one shot at a time."

Dard nodded. "The men have captured a number of the Furlorians who attempted to flee the village. They are bringing them to the town square now for your inspection."

Vort grinned. "That *is* good news, Commander. I knew I could count on *you*."

The commander waved Vort forward, and the soldiers gathered at their back, following a respectful distance behind as the pair made their way to the center of town. There, Vort sighed at seeing the few dozen furry aliens his men had corralled. It was hardly the numbers scanners had picked up on the *Monger*'s entry into the atmosphere.

"This is all of them?" he asked, shaking his head. "I'm beginning to think our men might need some measure of remedial training, Commander. Even on this primitive husk of a world, they can't contain the heathen locals fighting back with bolt weapons and hunting rifles? There were hundreds of these creatures nearby, and yet I can almost compare the number of dead and captured to your IQ. Why is this?"

The soldiers held their silence and forced the Furlorians to their knees in front of the captain. Vort strolled down the line of captives, glaring at each through his visor, watching with grim amusement as each looked away, staring at the ground to avoid meeting his gaze. The captain made three passes, letting his boots stomp heavily as he neared each alien, stirring up dust as he appraised them.

Clearly simple creatures, he assessed each as he walked past, deciding which of the furry aliens were most likely to surrender to Vort's whims should the creature be pushed. Several stood out as ones more likely to remain steadfast.

Clipped ears, scars across their cheeks or brows, missing whiskers or patches of fur torn loose ages ago, were signs of perseverance amongst the Furlorians. Those who'd undergone pain or cruel lives were far less likely to succumb to Vort's questioning.

Weak as the creatures appeared, Vort could see the defiance in their stiffened spines. They might not be willing to brave his stare, but there was no lack of courage or loyalty in the little aliens. They would not break as easily as he hoped.

As he made his third pass, he spotted one of the creatures trembling, doing its best to hide the tremors rattling its frame. Captain Vort stopped before the orangish-furred alien and leaned closer. He let out a loud exhalation of breath, his atmospheric filters releasing it with a low, serpentine hiss. He tapped the alien on the head, mussing its wild hair.

"This one is perfect," he told Dard. "Have it taken to the *Monger* and prepared for me." He glanced over at the rest of the Furlorians, who dared to peek past their fuzzy brows to see who among them had been chosen. Vort grinned in response to their curiosity, though he lamented the fact that they couldn't see how much their plight amused him. "Find a place here in town to house the rest until I tell you otherwise."

Commander Dard signaled, and two soldiers split from the group and grabbed the chosen Furlorian by the arms and hauled it away, its feet dragging behind it. Its brethren watched it being carted off as they themselves were herded together, arms bound behind their backs.

Vort marveled at their silence, even in the face of terror, yet he knew such stoicism would crumble once Vort turned his torturer loose upon their companion and they saw what had been done.

Vort knew all too well the locals had escaped his men, using their knowledge of the terrain to slip away, to hide, but he also knew he would find them soon enough. No matter what he had to do, he wouldn't let these little savages ruin his grand plans. Death would come for them all in time, and Vort would see his future elevated, at any cost.

"Prepare the drill teams, Commander. We've a planet to profit from."

CHAPTER TEN

Hands clasped Taj's arms and tugged at her. She howled and hissed, baring her teeth and lashing out with her claws. Her blood pumped hot through her veins, and her heart thundered like a storm rolling in over the plains. A loud ringing echoed in her ears, her own voice loud-, as it reverberated inside her skull. The aliens had killed Gran Beaux right before her. They wouldn't get her so easily.

"Easy, Taj, easy," a familiar voice grunted in her ear. "It's us," the voice said. "It's us."

Taj snarled and broke free from her captors, crouching, readying to lunge as her mind shook off the chaos rumbling inside her head. Tears blurred her vision, snot clogging her nose, but she caught a whiff of grease and fur, the familiar scents sending a calmness washing over her. She stumbled back another step and collided with the wall. Only Cabe's strong hands kept her from toppling over again.

"It's okay," he told her, pulling her in tight.

Taj stiffened and pushed him back. "No, it's not," she said, her voice raw, the words spewing out like sharpened knives. "They killed Beaux," she told them, "right in front of me. We need to—"

Cabe swallowed hard and grabbed her arm, reining her in before she could march off. "I know you want to avenge him," he started, his eyes shiny with barely repressed tears of his own, "we all do, but now is not the time."

"What do you mean?" she screeched back. "How is now not the time? They're right up there," she told him, pointing toward the hatch, "gloating over his corpse. Now is the *perfect* time."

He shook his head. "No, it's not."

Lina came alongside him, and she, too, looked ready to cry, her lower lip drawn into her mouth.

"Mama Merr is hurt bad, and she needs our help far more than Beaux does," Cabe said.

"How can you say that?" Taj slapped his hand from her arm and stepped back, growling low in her throat.

Torbon came forward, shaking his head. "You said they killed Beaux, right?"

"They did," she answered. "They threw two grenades at us, and he grabbed them before he slammed the hatch shut. H-he—"

Lina slipped by Torbon and wrapped her arms around Taj, hugging her tight. "We felt the explosion all the way down the tunnel when we were taking Mama to safety." She sucked in a deep breath, her chest shuddering as if she were choking on her next words. "He's dead, Taj. There's nothing you can do for him now. There's nothing anyone can do for him."

"No, he's—"

"Dead," Torbon finished for her, biting back his own sob. "He's dead, Taj, and Mama Merr will be also if we don't find a way to help her soon. I need to find Jadie, too, as soon as we can."

Taj hissed at him, the last of it gurgling away into a pained gasp. She'd watched Beaux cradle the grenades to his chest, heard him tell her to carry on with her life despite everything, watched him slam the hatch shut, and knew, without a doubt, the devices had exploded, giving him no time to escape. Not even she could have outrun them, and Beaux certainly couldn't, slow as he was.

He was dead.

Is *dead,* her mind corrected, and she hated herself for it. *Gone.*

She groaned and felt her legs threaten to give way beneath her, but she refused to fall, refused to surrender to the grief threatening to pull her under. She sunk her claws into the wall, tearing off tiny chips of stone as she righted herself.

Beaux had wanted her to take charge, wanted her to lead their people free of these aliens, to see them through the other side of this attack. He had spent his last breath telling her this, placing the mantle of the Furlorians on her shoulders, much as she hadn't wanted it. She sucked in a deep breath at the immensity of what she'd been tasked with. Beaux tasked *her* to lead their people, not the other Grans, not even Mama.

Her.

The weight of that loomed over her, pressing her down. Taj straightened and clenched her fists, ignoring the sharp tips of her claws biting into her palms. She met the eyes of each of her crew in turn, landing at last upon Cabe. Beaux had entrusted the future of the Furlorians to her, and she'd be damned if she let him down.

At last, she nodded, acknowledging that Beaux was gone, and nothing could be done for him except to honor his last wishes. That was how she could best serve him, avenge him, to make sure their people survived and kept on surviving.

"Let's get Mama," she told them, wiping her tears and snot away with the back of her hand. She marched down the tunnel in the direction she knew they'd taken her. "Then we can kill these alien gacks for all they've done."

The crew grunted their agreement and trailed after, their feet shuffling in the gloomy silence of the tunnel. Every footfall was a dirge.

Taj found Mama Merr in a small cubby hole deep inside the labyrinthine complex of narrow tunnels. Nearby, she could hear the muffled whispers of the townsfolk, voices carrying through the stony corridors. She fought the urge to shush them, certain the aliens couldn't possibly hear them, even if the whole of the Furlorian survivors shouted or cried out as one.

They were simply too deep to be detected, the makeup of the earth too dense and problematic for scanners to pierce accurately. They would be safe there unless the aliens stumbled across one of the secret entrances, and she had to hope they were hidden well enough to keep that from happening.

"Mama," Taj mumbled through trembling lips as she knelt beside the old Gran, running a hand over the woman's sweaty brow. "Can you hear me?"

Mama opened her eyes, a sliver of green showing through her lashes, and offered a shallow nod. "I can hear you, child," she answered, and to Taj's surprise, she did her best to force a smile. It was weak, hardly a glowbug's flicker against the sun's blazing light, but it was there. "Did we...all make...it?" she asked.

Taj's throat bobbed in response, battling the distasteful words that wanted to spill free of her mouth. Instead of telling Mama the truth, her eyes roamed the old queen's body, seeing the unnatural hitch to her back, and Taj lied. Lied like Beaux had.

Despite its justness, the decision would haunt her forever.

"Yes," she said, nodding her head, fearful she might fall over from her exuberance, the need to sell the fabrication to its fullest. "We're all here."

Mama's smile widened the slightest bit, and while Taj's heart threatened to burst, her dishonesty an incendiary wanting to go off, she was glad Mama didn't know the truth.

Taj could tell by the way she looked, the flutter of her eyes, the shallow, labored breaths she took, that Mama clung to the edge of life with a precarious grasp. Were she to learn how many of her people had failed to slip into the tunnels, that Gran Beaux had died helping Taj escape the aliens, it would kill the old Gran quicker than her injuries would. Of that, Taj was certain.

And maybe it was selfish of Taj to keep the truth from her, to lie and extend Mama's life a little longer for no reason other than that Taj needed, *wanted*, her there. Taj knew the truth would steal the last, best part of Mama away before she died: her hope. She couldn't do that to the old woman. She wouldn't break her heart.

"We need to get you somewhere safer, somewhere we can better evaluate your wounds and treat them."

Mama shook her head, her whiskers fluttering. "No, child, I've gone as far as I can manage." She reached out a gnarled paw and set it atop Taj's. Her claws scraped gently at her fur. "I know you want...to help, but there's none left for me."

She sucked in a breath, her whole body shaking at the effort. "My spine..." Mama started, spittle gleaming at her lips, "is broken, child. This here..." she patted the ground beside her, "is where I'll end my days, I'm afraid. Ain't nothing to be done about that."

So soon after Beaux, the world spun about Taj. She dropped to her butt, tears wiping out her vision, turning the old Gran into a hazy blur. The crew gathered around, and Taj could feel their presence looming over her shoulders. They'd all heard what Mama had said.

"No, don't think like that," Taj argued, though she, too, knew it to be the truth. They hadn't had the tech to repair such grievous injuries since long before they'd come to Krawlas. Herbs, splints, and the occasional splurge of energy to fuel the cryogen chambers aboard the freighters to slow a disease's creeping doom, but that was all there was.

With the aliens burning down Culvert City, the location of the old ships doubtlessly compromised already, they were down to the first two of the supplies. Neither of which would help a broken back, especially not in a queen as elderly as Mama Merr.

"There is no escaping the truth, child," Mama told her, and Taj nearly broke down at hearing the words so plainly spoken, as if Mama had pried into her brain and had seen Taj's deception. She clasped her hands about Mama's, afraid to squeeze but also afraid to let go. "However, while my time might well be coming to an end, there is still so much life for you and the others to live. I-I might not be here to see it, but I'll know my brood lives on in all of you."

Cabe set a hand on Taj's shoulder, clasping tight and holding her steady. She was grateful for it, fearful the spinning world would claim her and hurl her into the abyss of blackness nipping at her heart.

"We can't do this without you," Taj told her, still feeling like a million shards of glass, scattered to the sands after Beaux's passing. She couldn't stand to lose Mama, too. Not so soon. And while she knew it had to happen one day, there was no way she could handle it today, not after everything that had happened.

"You can, and you will, child," Mama answered. "You must, for our people. You are our future, and I would see us prevail, as we did before. The old die and young are born to carry on, and that's the cycle of it. You *will* continue on, no matter what happens to me or to the other Grans. You *will*."

Taj shifted sideways and wiped a glistening tear from her cheek with her shoulder. It gave her a chance to peel her eyes from Mama's and look to her crew. She imagined they looked much like her, wet-faced and somber, whiskers flat and ears pinned. She'd never seen them so forlorn, and she hated knowing they were seeing her just the same.

She wiped at her face again and looked back to Mama, doing her best to mimic stone, forcing her whiskers forward. "We'll gather some blankets to make you more comfortable," she told her, then reached out, slipping her hand into Cabe's pocket. She snatched his nip out before he realized what she was doing.

"Hey!" he cried out. "That's—" His argument ended before it started when he realized what Taj intended.

She peeled the back open and handed it to Mama. "Here. This will help a little with the pain."

Mama Merr cast a sideways glance at Cabe and managed a slightly disproving shake of her head, but she didn't refuse the offer. She took it in a wavering paw and lifted the open bag to her nose with help from Taj.

She sniffed deep and groaned, her nose dusted in nip, and then she leaned back against the stone, the emerald of her eyes like crescents of light behind the narrow gap of her lids. While there was no mistaking the agony she was in, there was the barest of reprieves playing out across her wrinkled face.

"Find someone to watch over her," Taj told Torbon, shooing him off. He left without complaint. "Lina, hunt for blankets and bring a few here, as many as can be spared." The engineer nodded and bolted down the tunnel, the pitter of her feet fading a moment later.

"What do you want me to do?" Cabe asked, and Taj shook her head.

"Stay here for now. I'm gonna need you soon enough."

Cabe nodded, though it was clear from his expression he wasn't sure what she was going to need him for. If she was being honest with herself, she wasn't sure either. Until she figured it out, though, she needed him there beside her, needed his solidness. Were she to be left alone with Mama, Taj knew she'd break down. She needed to be strong for Mama, for as long as she needed her to be.

Several quiet minutes later, the Gran's breaths slow and unsteady the entire time, Lina and Torbon returned. Several of the older townsfolk stood behind them: Gran Em, a woman nearly as old as Mama, born the runt of Mama's first litter; Harley, a young Furlorian who spent most of her time helping out in the kitchens and with the elderly; and Garr, a middle-aged Tom who'd been one of the first new litters born on Krawlas after the escape from Felinus 4.

"I couldn't find Jadie," Torbon said, concern causing his whiskers to droop a bit," but someone said they thought they'd seen her not long ago, helping people into the hatch."

"She's fine, Torbon. We'll find her, but if she's down here, she's safe."

Torbon drew in a deep breath and nodded. Taj wanted to comfort him, to reassure him, but Mama lay right before her, and there was little else Taj could think of right then. She snatched a blanket from Lina and wadded it up, easing it under Mama's head as Lina laid the others overtop the woman's frail body. Once the Gran was settled, Taj planted a kiss on the old queen's forehead.

Mama offered a whispered purr, the sound vibrating Taj's whiskers. "I love you, Mama," she whispered, her nose grazing Mama's cheek.

"And I you," the queen answered. "All of you." Her frail hand gestured toward the crew behind Taj. "B-be smart, children, and be strong. Help Beaux keep our people safe." Her eyes eased shut, and though Taj could still see her chest rising and falling, however shallowly, it felt to Taj as if Mama had spoken her last words. She hopped up and stormed off down the tunnel, the rest of the crew chasing after her as the others took their places beside Mama.

"Hey," Lina called out after a moment, running up behind Taj and grabbing her arm when she wouldn't stop. "What are you doing?"

"I need someplace to think, to plan," she answered.

"To plan what?" Torbon asked.

Taj spun about, her eyes rimmed with crimson fury. "How to kill each and every one of those gacking aliens who did this."

CHAPTER ELEVEN

Taj hid behind the stables, peeking out around the corner. The few pregnant balborans housed inside grumbled and paced, reacting to her presence and the smell of smoke from the burning buildings the aliens had laid waste to. Taj covered her mouth with her sleeve to keep from coughing and giving herself away.

A small band of alien soldiers paced the streets, standing guard over Culvert City and the five shuttles parked in a tight pack nearby, which had brought the soldiers to town from their ship.

The men's backs turned to her, and she had to fight the instinct to run up behind them and claw their throats out. Much as she wanted to, there were simply too many of them, and she didn't know if there were more inside the parked shuttles. She let out a quiet sigh and moved on. She had a job to do, and it didn't involve her getting killed.

At least not yet.

Taj waited until she was sure she wouldn't be seen, then

she scampered off. She darted across a side street and into an alley between the blacksmith's shop and the leatherworks shop, leaving the shuttles and soldiers behind. Once there, she pressed her back against the wall and peered back out at the aliens, again ensuring they weren't watching her. Their attention was mostly focused on the small ships.

Satisfied she was unseen, she made her way down the alley with careful, quiet steps, and then peered around the distant corner. Having only expected more of the same, scattered guards milling about, her heart sputtered at what she saw, and she flung herself backwards behind the wall again, panting.

There were fifty soldiers or more, armed and armored, and marching in a tight cluster, but that wasn't what had so worried her. Trapped in between the aliens were a bunch of her people, arms bound behind their backs and being made to trudge along with the soldiers, weapon barrels trained on them.

She knew them, knew them all, having lived and grown up there in Culvert City. These people were family, even if not by blood. She saw them nearly every day, chatted with them, went to class with them, danced and played with them. These were *her* people, and now they were in danger.

Taj's cheeks warmed, but she couldn't let her fury overwhelm her. Heavy-booted steps stomped her direction, and she knew they would soon pass by. She sucked in a harsh, quick breath, and ducked deeper into the alley, hunching down behind a barrel, which had been placed there at some point to catch the rain.

The stale scent of the water tickled her nose since it

hadn't been drained in a while, adding to the lurking waft of smoke. She sunk even lower, burying her face in her arm to avoid breathing it all in.

Not more than a moment later, the soldiers moved past. They shoved her captive people along none too kindly with rifle barrels. And while each and every one of them mattered, she spied a face she hadn't expected to see among the throng of captives.

Torbon's aunt, Jadie, the woman who'd raised him since he was a kitten.

Taj felt her chest tighten at the sight of her, sickened by the thought that she'd dismissed Torbon's concern, assuring him Jadie was fine, even though Taj didn't know a gacking thing about what had happened to her. She'd simply been caught up in her own grief, too walled off to take stock of Torbon's. She groaned under her breath, hating herself right then, knowing how important Jadie was to her friend.

Though Taj knew everyone being ushered away, it was even harder to watch Jadie being herded like a balboran calf because she was real family, Torbon's blood. She was the only person directly related to any of the crew left alive these days. It would kill Torbon to know she hadn't slipped into the tunnels as he'd been told.

And like the others, she looked beaten, eyes downcast as they were pushed along. A few Furlorians, mostly the younger ones, sniffled at their plight. The majority, however, held a defiant silence, not willing to give their captors any pleasure.

Taj growled low, muffling the sound against her hand, understanding there was nothing she could do yet, but that didn't stop her from imagining the retribution she would claw from their hides the first opportunity that prevented itself. A grim smile peeled her lips back. She swore on Beaux's memory these invaders would pay, and that she'd free Torbon's aunt right along with all the others.

Once all the aliens had moved on, Taj made her way to the corner once more and watched the crowd until it disappeared from sight. Then she started after them, slipping from building to building, staying to the shadows as best she could so she wouldn't be spotted.

She needn't have worried. The soldiers were focused on their hostages, a victorious swagger in their steps. As far as they were concerned, the fight was over, the planet conquered.

Taj snarled at the presumption. For her, the war had just begun.

The aliens marched on through town for a while, and Taj realized where they were going. With the downed enemy ship in the opposite direction, and nothing else out that way but open fields, the distant balboran pens, and the trio of barns where her people stored the hay and feed for the balborans during the winter, there was nowhere else to go.

Right now, the barns were empty and would make the perfect location to stash the Furlorians away. The fact that all the doors were hanging open told her the aliens had already scouted the area and clearly knew that.

A lump formed in Taj's throat when she realized the aliens' intent as they shepherded her people into the nearest of the barns before slamming the doors shut behind them. The aliens must have realized they hadn't captured or killed all the Furlorians and planned to hold the ones they had caught as leverage against the others. That didn't bode well, but at least it meant there was still time to do something.

She stared as a dozen of the soldiers fanned out and encircled the barn, positioning themselves so there were no real gaps between their stations for someone to slip past unseen. Taj sighed, recognizing that the aliens knew she and other Furlorians would come for their brethren, and the invaders were prepared to keep that from happening.

A cold chill prickled at her skin as she watched the remainder of the soldiers turn and march back the way they'd come, right toward her again. She hissed and darted back into another alley, hiding once more until they were gone. She hunkered in the trash for a few minutes to be sure they weren't lurking about.

Her legs pulsed with the start of cramps, the stealthy back and forth and hiding using muscles she was unused to using, especially after the rough ride of the last few hours. Taj grunted and clambered back to her feet.

A shuffle at the end of the alley drew her up short.

She stiffened, her hand yanking the bolt pistol from its holster and raising the barrel as she turned toward the source of the sound. Though she was prepared to, she hoped she wouldn't have to use the it. While the aliens deserved every hole she punched through them, she knew the noise of gunfire would draw the rests of the soldiers to her.

Essentially surrounded on all sides, there'd be no getting out of town if she was forced into a battle here and now. So, instead, she bared her fangs and crept toward the front of the alley, claws ready to do as much damage as she could silently.

The scrape sounded again, and a dark figure eked around the corner and pressed itself against the wall, the shadows obscuring it. Taj stepped up, raised the pistol, and aimed it at the figure's head, then laid her claws against the figure's throat as she caught a scent she recognized.

"You almost got yourself shot," she whispered, sheathing her claws.

Cabe started, and she slapped her hand over his mouth to muffle the squawk of surprise he let out. His eyes shot wide over her paw, and Taj could see his heartbeat thumping at his temple. Only when his eyes narrowed, and he exhaled warmly into her palm in relief, shoulders slumping, did she remove her hand from his mouth.

"You wouldn't have needed the gun," he mumbled. "You damn near gave me a heart attack."

"Good," she told him. "You deserve it for following me. Why are you here?"

He met her gaze, though she could see he fought the urge to drop his chin to his chest and look away as he'd done so many times while Mama Merr scolded him when he was a kitten.

"I know you told me to stay with the others, with Mama, but I didn't want you out here by yourself."

"I'm hardly alone," she told him, grabbing his arm and leading him to the other end of the alley. With an extended claw, she motioned for him to look around the corner.

Cabe looked around and drew back a second later, eyes wide once more. "Gacking Rowl! They're everywhere."

She nodded. "They're gathering up our people. They

have Jadie, too," she said, a jagged edge to her voice. "There's a bunch of them in the barn over there." She jabbed a claw in the general direction. "I'm worried about them."

Cabe swallowed hard and nodded. Taj could tell by the wrinkled expression on his face that he understood why the aliens had collected their people. Nothing good would come of it. "What are we gonna do?"

Taj shrugged. "I know what I want to do, but there are so many of these gacking aliens. Even if all our people were free to fight, I'm not sure we could take them." She let out a weary sigh, the pulses of anger that had so consumed her earlier, now cooling in the wake of what appeared to be impossible odds. "Still, we need to."

"Yeah," Cabe agreed as if by instinct, but she could tell he was unsure.

There was no questioning his loyalty or courage, but Taj understood what they were up against, and so did he. This was no simulation, no holo-remembrance of a war long relegated to the past. No, this was a new war, *their* war. There'd be no heroes swooping in and rescuing them from the bad guys, no last-minute saviors to sacrifice themselves for the Furlorians' future. This fight was on them.

As were the consequences of failure.

Taj listened to the voices in her head, every one of them screaming for her to flee, to find someplace to hide until the aliens finally got whatever they came for and left, returning to the stars.

The voices wanted nothing to do with these aliens. They'd killed Beaux, crippled—and likely killed—Mama, too. They'd killed many more of her people, too many for Taj to name, and captured Jadie, Torbon's aunt and the others. There was nothing but death waiting if she were to ignore the good sense the voices spewed.

Run.

Hide.

Escape.

Live!

Taj drew in a deep breath and let it out slow. Her mind was already made up. "Gack the voices."

"Huh?" Cabe asked, oblivious to the arguments and chaos reverberating inside her skull.

"We can't beat these bastards head-on," she started, "but that doesn't mean we can't hurt them or make them pay for what they've done."

"How do you suggest we do that?"

She forced a grin, eyeteeth gleaming in the gloom. "We fight dirty, that's how."

CHAPTER TWELVE

"You sure about this?" Torbon asked, shaking his head as he watched Lina tinker with the damaged windrider, the *Thorn* stashed away behind a dune outside of Culvert City.

"Am I *sure*?" Taj countered, emphasizing the question with a shrug. "I'm not *sure* of anything." Thoughts of Torbon's aunt popped into her head, but she shrugged them off. She hadn't told him she'd seen her, that Jadie was a captive. That was another decision she was unsure of, but she needed Torbon focused on the task at hand. "Still, these aliens aren't exactly giving us much in the way of options, Torbon. We have to do *something*."

"I know that, but do you really think this is the best way to go about this?"

"Again, you're asking me a question I don't have an answer to," she told him. "I'm making all this up as I go along. These aliens have our friends, our families..." she said, hesitating to tell him she'd seen Jadie. "Judging by how they rolled into town, shooting first and saying nothing, it's clear they don't place much value on our lives."

"That's exactly my point, Taj. It's clear they don't care, but shouldn't we?"

"So, you're saying we should run away and let them kill everyone?" Lina asked, spitting the words out before Taj could.

Torbon shook his head. "I'm not saying that at all, but we have to be smart here."

"We do," Taj replied, "but we also need to be decisive. There is absolutely no reason for these aliens to take hostages if they don't intend to use them for something. Whether that something is to lure the rest of us in, for slave labor of some kind, or Rowl knows what else, they have something in mind. As soon as our people stop being useful, then what?"

Torbon only stared, but she could see the sense of what she was saying was sinking in. "They're gonna kill them, Torbon, unless we do something about it." She pictured Torbon watching Jadie die and shook her head to clear the image. There was enough guilt piling up already.

"But this?" He pointed at the *Thorn*, the tiny craft battered from their last encounter with the aliens, a half-dozen external fuel tanks connected to its hull and running down the wings. "How is this gonna help?"

Taj grinned. "Watch and see."

He sighed. "You know I hate when you say that."

"Me, too," Lina said, joining in. "I'm not really sure we should do this either. What happens afterward?"

"We move on to plan B," Taj replied.

"And after that?"

"Plans C through the rest of the alphabet get dragged out until we either win or die, whichever happens first," Taj said, raising her hands as if the answer had been obvious.

"I am *sooooo* inspired now," Cabe said, crossing his arms over his chest with a huff. "Probably should have let the trrilacs kill us. At least that would have been an accident. *This*…this is suicide."

"Got a better idea?" Taj asked.

"*Better* is subjective," he answered. "*Smarter*, certainly."

"Will it help us free our people?"

He spit a mouthful of brownish juice onto the sand and unconsciously rubbed the slight bump at his jaw where he always held a wadded mass of nip between his cheek and teeth.

He might have given up his stash to Mama, but he still had a mouthful he apparently clung to with almost religious fervor. "No, but my idea will stop Torbon's stomach from rumbling and my tail from poofing so badly every time I hear a gacking sound."

"So, your idea is to run away and eat?" Taj asked.

Cabe grunted. "It's a work in progress, I'll admit. Rough outline."

"Lunch is always a good idea," Torbon added, rubbing his belly. "We should go with Cabe's plan."

Taj groaned, and Lina did her best not to laugh, burying her head inside one of the windrider's maintenance compartments to finish her work.

"We'll eat when our people are safe," Taj told them, glaring at each in turn until they looked away from her withering gaze. "Until then, we do things my way."

"Your way sucks because it doesn't involve snacks," Torbon said quietly, muffling his words behind a paw.

Taj ignored him and glanced over at Lina, who'd popped her head free of the ship. "Almost ready?"

Lina nodded and held up a small device, two red lights flickering on its face. She tossed the metal box to Cabe. He caught it gingerly and stared at it as if it might bite him.

"The stabilizer fix gonna hold?" Taj asked.

Lina shrugged. "It's held together with spit and snot, so who knows, but it should keep it together long enough to do what needs to be done."

"Rowl, but I hate having to do this," Cabe muttered.

"Me, too, but I'm sure it will work," Taj told him.

"Oh, now you're *sure*?" Torbon said.

Taj hissed at him, and Torbon ducked behind the bulkier Cabe in case she did more than that. She didn't, not bothering with him. She had more than enough to worry about without adding Torbon's childish inanity to the pile.

Once she committed to her plan, there would be no peace for any of them. Succeed or fail, the fight was on as soon as she signaled Cabe to get on with it. Could she live with the consequences?

I'll have to, she thought.

"No going back now," she said, staring out over her crew.

They'd been together since they were kittens. While they weren't of the same litter, they couldn't be any closer if they had been. All four of them had grown up together, been weened together, taught how to fight and survive together. Now, if they were going to die, at least they'd do that together, too. Though, she had to admit, that last part was small consolation.

"Do it," she ordered before she could change her mind, hoping Cabe would follow through without argument.

Gratefully, he did.

Cabe sighed and stared at the device, familiarizing himself with it quickly, not that there was much to it. A button, a switch, two lights, and a tiny, makeshift joystick. His upper lip peeled back as he stared at the metal box, then he shook his head and flipped the switch. The two lights changed from red to green, and the windrider rumbled to life in response.

"No going back now," he parroted and kissed his palm, pressing his hand against the hull of the windrider. "I'll miss you, girl. Go with Rowl." The words barely out of his mouth, he thumbed the joystick. The *Thorn* sputtered and rose into the air with a rattling tremor. "Get ready to run," he told them, then he moved the stick forward.

The windrider coughed, spitting black smoke from its engines, then shot forward, spinning in a circle once more, as it had the last time they'd ridden on it.

The small craft shot off, zipping low over the tops of the scruffy dunes, kicking up clouds of dust with its wild arc. Without the weight of the crew aboard, it moved faster than Taj had ever remembered seeing it. That was both good and bad.

Good that it would pick up all the speed it needed. Bad because it left them exposed, no hiding where the craft came from. She held her breath as it hurtled over the sandy earth, praying to Rowl for guidance. As much as she believed she was doing the right thing, this one act would change everything.

The crew darted off, staying low behind the dunes as the *Thorn* flew faster and faster toward its target. Taj knew it would only be a matter of seconds before the aliens realized what was going on, and as she thought that, she heard the sudden flaring of alarms in the distance. She offered a bitter grin at the sound, knowing it was too late for anyone to do anything.

She sighed and peeked out between a pair of narrow dunes, slowing so she could watch the fallout of her actions. A lot of pressure rested on her shoulders now that Beaux was gone, and she needed to prove herself. Her breath caught in her lungs as the first of her battle plans came to fruition. She'd know soon enough if she'd succeeded.

The *Thorn* streaked over the last of the sandy rises, and Cabe brought it in low, letting it skim a short distance above the ground. Blaster fire erupted from the aliens gathered about, but the small arms fire wasn't enough to bring down the windrider. Taj smiled as she watched the alien soldiers panic and scatter as the *Thorn* closed on them.

There was no stopping it now.

Lina whooped as the *Thorn* struck its target: the first of the alien shuttles parked together in a regimental line with little room between them.

The windrider smashed into the side of the enemy shuttle, its momentum driving it through the thin frame and out the other side. Fuel trailed from the exterior tanks punctured by the impact, debris scattered about.

The *Thorn* struck the second shuttle a heartbeat later, but it had been slowed enough by the first collision that it barely managed to puncture the side. It slammed to a halt inside the other craft, which slid into the third of the shuttles. Sparks flew as metal clanged against metal.

That's when the extra fuel ignited.

The *Thorn* exploded right after, fire and fury bursting loose of its constraints. The shuttle it rested inside exploded right along with it, adding its fuel and weaponry to the volatile mixture.

The first shuttle burst into flames next, followed by the third as it was doused with wreckage and streams of fiery fuel. Flame hurtled past the other two shuttles parked nearby, scorching the ships black.

Those soldiers who hadn't seen the windrider coming were consumed in the conflagration right alongside the ships. Aliens shrieked as the flames licked at them, boiling them inside their armor before they'd managed to get more than a few steps from the exploding crafts. Bodies dropped, smoldering shadows amidst the orange-red blaze. A dozen aliens ran screaming, streaks of flame urging them on.

The fourth shuttle caught fire, and Taj heard muffled *thumps* reverberate inside it, its hull warping dramatically. Then it toppled to its side, a gout of fire jetting free from the front landing gear port, twisting and warping the gear until it gave way. The ship crashed into the dirt and kicked up a cloud of dust and sand, showering the last of the shuttles, dousing what little flames had reached it.

That probably kept it from exploding, Taj thought,

watching from her vantage point between the distant dunes. *We need to do something about that—*

Her thought went unfinished as the engines of the last shuttle flared to life, and it rose into the sky, veering away from the others at a sharp angle. The ship straightened a moment later, and Taj heard its engines bark as the pilot accelerated hard. The shuttle shot straight toward them.

"Gack!" Cabe shouted. "That pilot's good."

"Admire him later," Taj shouted back. "Run now!"

Torbon had already bolted, with Lina at his heels. Cabe nodded and chased after the pair, and Taj ran, putting everything she had into the effort. Still, she didn't think it would be enough.

The roar of the shuttle grew closer and closer, the sound eclipsing the explosions rocking the others, and she knew that, at any moment, she and her crew would be gunned down. While the weaponry on the shuttles were limited to a couple of forward-facing guns, they were more than sufficient to kill them without much effort.

Fortunately, she had planned ahead.

She'd been unable to get the crew to hide out and wait for her to launch the *Thorn* on her own before running back to meet her. Their stubbornness was as bad as hers. But she'd at least been able to convince them to prepare a primitive hidey hole ahead of time.

She darted around the nearest dune and saw Torbon, who'd arrived first, yank the edge of a camouflaged tarp back at the base of the dune. He waved Lina under it. Cabe grabbed the edge from him and pushed Torbon under before holding it for Taj.

"Get under cover already," she shouted at him.

He shook his head. "I'm faster than you," he told her, waving her on as the rumbling sound of the shuttle grew closer and closer. "If they spot someone, it's best it's me so I can lure them away."

Taj growled, but she didn't argue. There simply wasn't time for debate. The shuttle was over the rise, already kicking up dust to signal its approach, peppering them with dirt.

Rather than wait for him to slip in after her, Taj dove into a roll. Cabe's eyes went wide when he realized what she was doing, but it was too late. She crashed into his legs and wrapped around them, locking her hands together. Cabe hissed, but there was no stopping her.

The two, tangled together with limbs flailing, rolled under the tarp and slammed into the other two, knocking them all into the sandy base of the dune. The tarp fluttered behind them and dropped to the ground, wavering in the breeze the shuttle was causing.

Taj disengaged from Cabe and dove for the tarp as the shuttle broke over the rise. Her claws snagged the material, and she pulled it tight against the ground, submerging the edge in the sandy ground to keep it from being seen. Dirt spun all around outside, caught up in the shuttle's wake, and Taj felt its weight settling on the tarp, helping to hold it in place and better conceal it.

Still, they weren't safe yet.

While she'd prepared for the potential of a shuttle or two surviving her destructive plan, she knew how flimsy a hideout they were pinning their hopes on. A stray gust of wind from the shuttle's passing could easily rip the tarp loose of the sand and her grip, exposing them to the enemy.

Worse still, a level-headed pilot would rely on more than his own eyes to track down the people responsible for the attack on the shuttles. Were he to bring up his sensors and do a solid sweep of the area, the tarp would do nothing to deflect the scan.

The crew would be exposed, and in a position where they had no chance of escape. And it seemed the pilot was getting ready to do just that. The shuttle seemed to slow and hover above the dunes, the pilot clearly rationalizing his course of action.

"Do it now," Taj whispered to Lina, waving a hand behind her.

Fortunately, Taj had planned to sow a little more dissension to keep the aliens distracted.

Lina pulled a second, smaller device from her uniform pocket and flipped a silver switch. A red light appeared, then it turned to green. She pressed the sole button on the side, and a distant *whump* resounded in response.

The shuttles engine's wailed, and a wall of wind buffeted the tarp as the alien ship shot away, roaring toward the distant explosion, which Taj knew had shot black smoke into the sky.

She waited a moment, barely giving the shuttle time to depart, before she whipped the tarp away and jumped to her feet. "Let's go." Taj started off without a glance back, circling the nearest dune and bolting for the old tunnel entrance that had been hidden way out into the desert ages back.

With the shuttle pilot focused on the bait explosion

they'd triggered, there was time to reach the entrance and slip away before the aliens realized they'd been tricked.

Taj sighed as she ran. While the aliens had fallen for it this time, she knew they'd be better prepared the next time. More importantly, she understood there would be consequences for their actions. The aliens would not take kindly to their shuttles being blown up. Already hostile, she could only imagine what their first reaction would be.

Taj could only hope none of the townspeople would be hurt by her actions. While she knew the aliens would react poorly and would be looking for vengeance, she wasn't sure she was ready to live with blood on her hands like Mama Merr had talked about.

It was one thing to be killed doing what Taj felt was right. It was another entirely to get someone else killed for it.

CHAPTER THIRTEEN

"The locals did what?" Captain Vort screamed at the soldier prostrated on his knees before him.

"Uh, they—"

Vort didn't let the man finish. He smashed his armored knee into the soldier's visor, knocking him onto his back. A spider web of cracks covered the man's face mask, and Vort took advantage of his inability to see.

The captain raised a boot and brought it down on the soldier's head. Then he did it again and again, repeatedly slamming the soldier's helmet into the dirt. The man screamed and begged for mercy, only infuriating Vort more.

"Don't you dare say another word!" the captain shouted, dropping his full weight onto the man's chest.

Cheeks burning like embers, he grabbed the hoses running from the soldier's helmet and tore them free. A burst of steam exploded free, wetting his hand as Vort wrapped the hoses around his fist.

He yanked hard, pulling the man's helmet off. The soldier gasped as the steam that carried moisture into the soldier's lungs was yanked away, exposing him to the dry, desert air. Vort didn't give him a chance to catch his breath or adjust.

The captain raised the man's helmet and brought it down on the soldier's face. The tell-tale *snap* of bone breaking echoed loudly, but that didn't stop Vort. He repeatedly slammed the helmet into the soldier's face until there was nothing left but a bloody puddle where his head had been only moments before. Even then, Vort didn't stop, slamming the helmet down, spattering himself and anyone near with warm and bloody viscera, every blow landing with a wet splash.

"I believe he's dead, Captain," Commander Dard said, though even he knew well enough not to attempt to physically stop the captain's onslaught.

"He's dead when I say he's dead," Vort replied, bringing the helmet down another couple of times until it sunk into a crevice he'd created in the ground below the soldier's shattered skull. Vort grunted and drew in a deep breath, shaking the helmet free of his hand and tossing it aside. "*Now* he's dead."

"Of course," Dard replied, his voice deadpan. "I'll have the men clear the body away."

"No," the captain shouted. "Leave him here as a reminder to the others. I will *not* abide their stupidity."

Commander Dard barked an affirmative.

Vort clambered to his feet, shaking his hand, sending blood and gore flying everywhere. He spun on the commander, every breath heavy even through the voice modulator of his visor. "How is it possible for furry little rats to take out four of our five shuttles in one attack?"

"It would appear the pilots expected no resistance, sir. They parked the shuttles in line, as they would at home, allowing the locals to strike them at once." He gestured toward the glowing ruin of the shuttles. "While three of the crafts are destroyed, a fourth suffered only minor damage and can be righted and repaired promptly. The fifth survived with only cosmetic damage, and the pilot was able to take flight and follow the attackers from the air."

"And those attackers?" Vort asked. "Are their corpses withering out in the desert, shot full of holes and waiting for my appraisal, Commander?"

Dard swallowed hard. "They, uh, appear to have escaped him, sir."

"Of course, they have." Captain Vort grunted and spun about, facing the soldiers gathered around him. "This is the second time these rodents have made fools of us...of *you*," he said, jabbing a finger at his men. "There had better not be a third time. Do I make myself clear?" He glanced at the wreckage of the soldier he'd killed in emphasis.

"Sir, yes, sir!" the men replied in unison, their enthusiasm remotely positive, at least.

"We are at war," he reminded them, "no matter the strength of the resistance. We will stand at war-facing at all times. Understood?"

"Sir, yes, sir!" they repeated, their exuberance upped a notch from their last response.

Vort, knowing his men would say anything he wanted them to in order to avoid being the next gooey stain in the dirt, turned to face Dard. At least the commander would offer an honest answer. "Will these locals continue to be a threat to our operations?"

Dard hesitated a moment, and then offered a sharp nod. "While I hate to suggest they might, as few as there are, and as disorganized as they might be, I believe they will. They are, after all, fighting for their lives, their very existence, and their home world. Would you roll over so easily for an invader, Captain?"

Vort chuckled. He knew damn well he wouldn't. The captain remained silent a moment, looking about, letting his gaze linger on an invisible point near the far side of the town where he knew the alien hostages were being held.

"No, of course, I wouldn't," he confirmed. "However, I am nothing like these savages. I know full well the power of attachment and have spent my life avoiding such foolish pitfalls, ensuring I had no one to be used against me."

Vort grinned behind his helmet, and while he knew Commander Dard couldn't see it, he was certain the man could feel the pleasure wafting off him. "In a town this small, what are the odds that our would-be guerillas are related to some of those we have stashed away in that dilapidated barn?"

"I'd think the odds are quite favorable, Captain. They are an incestuous species, after all."

"Indeed, they are, Commander," Vort replied. "So, rather than spend our time hunting a few small rats hiding in a huge desert, I suggest we set out some bait to lure them to us."

"That sounds like a perfect idea."

"Of course, it is, Commander. I thought of it." Vort chuckled. "Now, let's go and set some traps, shall we?"

CHAPTER FOURTEEN

Taj hunkered down behind the parapet that encircled Culvert City's lone entertainment venue, a weathered building built like an old matinee theater the owner had once seen in a holo-vid. The place served as a gathering place for the younger Furlorians. They'd get together and scamper through the place as vintage holos played on a great white screen at the far end of the room.

Set at the edge of town, opposite the barns, it drew all the rangier Furlorians in because they could be as loud as they wanted to be without disturbing the Grans or the balborans penned on the other side of town.

Tonight, the twin moons of Krawlas staring down at them with an orangish gaze, Taj sat alongside the rest of her crew and looked out over the town with a pair of gazefinders, slowly adjusting the lens focus on the side.

"What do you see?" Lina asked, her tail *fwapping* against the wood of the roof.

Taj had chosen the location because it provided the

clearest view of the town while still providing them with adequate cover not to be seen in return. She waved a hand to hush Lina, swinging her gaze down the alleys and streets, trailing the loose groups of alien soldiers who made their rounds through the city.

"Not much," she finally answered. "Patrols sweep through regularly, but they don't seem to have a specific route they stick to. Lots of ad lib adjustments, a couple of soldiers veering off from a group to explore an alley and meet back up around the other side, while some randomly stop and go back the way they've come."

She sighed and thumped her forehead against the parapet. "As disorganized as it looks, this random gack is gonna keep us from sneaking around town since we can never be sure where they're gonna be minute by minute."

"So, we're screwed." Torbon said. "What now?"

"Same plan, different approach," Cabe answered.

Taj and Lina nodded in unison. "Exactly. It's way too early for us to quit. I think we can—" She drew in a sharp, quick breath. "Wait!" With a trembling claw, she pointed into the distance. "There's a bunch of them coming this way." She shook the gazefinders and grumbled at its limitations, the commotion in the distance little more than a blur. "I can't see well enough to know what's going on. We're gonna have to wait."

"That's all we've *been* doing," Torbon grumbled.

Taj couldn't disagree. Her idea to wreck the shuttles had been a good one, but she knew it was hardly a match held up the raging inferno of what they were getting into. The enemy had the numbers and had hostages. They most likely had experience on their side, too, seeing how she and the crew were nothing more than kids playing at war.

Taj wanted to tell Torbon she had some grand plan of action, some failproof idea that would see them and their people through this, but she didn't have gack. Taj gulped as the gazefinder's view cleared, and she realized how little she was prepared for all this.

The alien commander's arrival in town square with an armed and armored squadron of soldiers and a handful of shackled Furlorians hammered that reality home. Worse still, her eyes scanned over the assemblage and caught Jadie's sad features among the clustered people the aliens had dragged from their makeshift prison.

"Oh..." The gazefinders tumbled from numb fingers, and Torbon snatched them out of the air before they hit the roof.

"Let me see," he muttered, nudging Taj aside and peering out over the parapet.

"I don't think that's a—" That was all Taj got out before Torbon stiffened and *mrowled* low, the sound rumbling in his throat. "Bloody Rowl," she finished, realizing Torbon had caught sight of his aunt.

A hand shot out to his side and grabbed Taj's arm tightly, claws digging in. "They'd got Jadie!" He stuffed the gazefinders in Lina's stomach, the girl barely able to latch onto them, before he shot upright. "We've got to do something!"

Cabe grabbed him by the shoulders and pulled him down. "Not now," Cabe hissed.

Torbon shrugged free, spinning about and leaning in so closely to Cabe that their noses touched. "Then when,

Cabe? When?" And just as quickly as before, he spun about again, glaring out toward where the aliens held his aunt. "Do you really think they brought them out here to play nice?"

Taj groaned, hating that her normally daft friend had picked up on exactly the same thing she had the moment the aliens had trotted their fellow Furlorians out into the town square. This was retribution for the shuttles, a lesson to her and the crew.

"No," Cabe replied, grabbing ahold of Torbon once more, this time clearly doing it to keep him from breaking loose. "They're there to lure us out so they can kill all of us, Torbon."

Torbon growled, but before he could respond, a mass of bright lights erupted in the town square, night instantly turning to day, and then the amplified voice of the alien commander echoed through town.

"Denizens of Krawlas, I am Captain Relius Vort of the *Monger*, a destroyer in the grand Navy of the Wyyvan Empire. Were I you, I would listen closely to my proclamation and take close heed, for I will not repeat myself."

Cabe wrestled Torbon to the rooftop, sitting down behind him and locking his legs and arms around the other Tom. Torbon grunted and moaned, but there was little he could do against the applied strength of Cabe. After a moment, he settled in to listen, staring out through the rails of the parapet. The rest of the crew watched with their last breath clutching to their lungs.

"Now that I have your attention..." The enemy captain drew a pistol and pressed it against the head of a Tom they'd dragged out into the square. Without warning, the alien pulled the trigger.

There was a muffled *thwump* as energy met skull, and the blast won out.

The Tom's eyes went wide before his face exploded, and he crumpled to the ground, the place where his head had been now nothing more than a smoking crater.

Taj managed to slap a hand over Torbon's mouth as he screamed, the sound buried in his mouth behind her palm. He squirmed and fought, but Cabe held him fast, managing to rein him in as the alien captain started speaking again.

Vort stepped over the body of the dead Furlorian and pulled another one to his side. "While I understand we got off to a bad start, my overzealous men firing on your people without provocation, we are beyond that now. The situation's changed. Our landing here was an accident, but as it turns out, it was one of great providence. There is a great source of energy embedded in this planet, making it invaluable to myself and my masters. And while I might have approached you differently before our discovery, it has surely changed things."

"Yeah, we can see that," Lina muttered, hands whitening as she gripped the rail tight. Taj hushed her as the captain continued.

"I will, however, offer a form of mercy to you and yours," he said. "Should each and every one of you turn yourself into me and my men, I will be lenient. I will kill no more of you should you submit. And when our mission here is done, the mineral stripped from the planet—a mineral, I might add, that you clearly make no use of or likely even knew existed—me and my people will then leave you to your planet, alive and unharmed."

"And he expects us to believe that," Cabe said with a growl. "He murdered one of our people right in front of us."

Taj nodded, unable to agree more. She knew damn well the captain, Vort as he called himself, wanted nothing more than to bring the Furlorians under his thumb, to capture and contain them, and worse, likely kill them all so they didn't get in his way.

Right now, though Taj had no idea how many of her people were still free and capable of fighting back, she knew it would only be a matter of time until the aliens pressed their advantage and killed them all.

"The alternative, however…" He shot another Tom in the back, dumping his scorched body into the dirt. "Do I make myself clear?" He spun in a circle, addressing an audience no one could see.

Taj imagined she could smell the charred skin from where they cowered. Her whiskers peeled back in disgust.

Torbon squeaked and started fighting again. Jadie was next in line.

Right then, a whisper of a voice called out from the opposite side of the square. Three Toms and a queen slunk out of the shadows, hands in the air. "We're here!" Taj recognized the Tom as Hugh, or Squirreltail, as he was nicknamed because of his tendency to puff up at the slightest provocation.

He limped toward the captain, his entourage following his flared tail, and soldiers swirled around, guns pointed their direction. "We're here; don't shoot."

Taj could almost hear the grin in Vort's voice. "Yes, bring them here. Let them join their brethren here in the circle."

The soldiers grabbed the free Furlorians as soon as they approached, binding them the same they had the others, pushing them together. The captain stared the newcomers down for a moment, then patted one on the head before walking in a slow circle around the gathered captives.

"See that wasn't so complicated, was it?" he asked, waving his pistol in the air. "Still, I know there are more of you watching this display and hesitating to do as your courageous companions here have done. But understand this. I am a Wyyvan of my word, both the good and bad ones, be assured."

He paced around the gathering and stopped in front of them, facing the main part of town. "Now, I will let my example sink in for now and let those of you still unsure of your choice, time to think it over. Tomorrow night, at this same time, we will return with five more captives. Not those wise enough to have surrendered tonight, of course, and we will do this all over again. Should no others submit to us, we will kill one of the hostages we've dragged out here every few minutes until they are all dead. Then, the day after, we'll do it again, and so on and so forth, day after day until there are no more of you left."

A quiet chuckle spilled through the amplifiers sending his voice echoing through town. "Be smart and turn yourself in. The only real choice you have is surrender or death. Make it easy on yourselves and choose the former." He spun on a heel and marched off.

The soldiers gathered the captives and pushed them

into a tight group and stomped after their commander, the hostages herded along with them as they had been earlier.

Taj swallowed hard and sucked in a lungful of air once they were gone, not having realized she'd been holding her breath. She slumped against the railing, legs trembling, heart fluttering.

A sob broke from Torbon as soon as Taj's hand slipped away. His eyes glistened with tears. "They have Jadie. We need to do something."

Cabe hugged him, and Taj dropped down beside him, joining the embrace. Lina hovered, her own eyes shiny with tears. Taj met his wavering gaze, though it was hard to do given that she'd known they had Jadie and hadn't told Torbon. She knew exactly how he'd react; just like she would have. Still, she'd kept it from him, and the guilt gnawed at her conscience.

She knew there was nothing more to do than what they were working on already, but that was hardly consolation. Taj knew if it were Mama being held captive, nothing on Krawlas could hold her back from trying to rescue her. Was it right that she stop Torbon from doing the same?

No, it wasn't right, but it was smart.

At least she told herself that.

"We'll get her back," she told him. "I promise."

Torbon sniffed, slipping a newly freed hand away from Cabe to wipe his nose. "Can you promise that, Taj?" he asked. "Can you really?"

She sighed, knowing damn well it was an empty promise, just as he did. Pretty words to soften the truth she had grasp of.

No, she couldn't promise Torbon anything beyond this:

"I can promise I won't stop trying to free her as long as I live, Torbon."

He stared at her, their eyes near to boiling, before he dropped his gaze and sniffed. He said nothing, but there was no mistaking the jagged edges of his posture. Though she couldn't read his mind, she knew gacking well what he was thinking.

He didn't believe her, even though he wanted to. It wasn't going to happen, and she couldn't blame him.

They were all in over their heads, barely managing to catch a breath or two as the calamitous waves washed over. The aliens held the upper hand in every way that mattered: men, guns, armor, and experience. All Taj and her crew had was determination. And while that might well be a great help in sporting competition, this was war.

Life and death hung in the balance, and as the poor Furlorians who'd done nothing but stand there as the enemy circled—and now whose bodies laid limp in the town square, unburied, un-mourned—it was clear which way the pendulum swung at the moment.

If the crew were to stay and fight, it would likely be the last action of their young lives. Would their defiance alone make a difference?

That was the question Taj wrestled with. Still, she couldn't see Beaux or Mama surrendering to these alien invaders. They'd battled to escape Felinus 4, sacrificing everything they had, their homes, their families, their *everything*, in order to ensure the Furlorian race would survive, the bloodline continuing on into the future. And though Gran Beaux was gone, nuzzling into Rowl's side, and Mama was clinging to life by a weary claw, she knew they had expectations of her.

The two hadn't sneaked away in the dark, saving their immediate family and vanishing from Felinus 4. No, they'd risked their lives, fought to free and rescue as many of their people as they possibly could, losing friends and loved ones in the process.

Yet the two never complained about what they'd sacrificed to see the rest of the Furlorians here to Krawlas, to safety. Not once that Taj could remember. No, they'd been proud of what they'd done, and they'd have sacrificed even more to have done what they did, up to and including their own lives.

Taj snarled and stared out at the dead bodies littering the town square. If death awaited her, so be it. She would see Jadie and the others free, or they would all die in the attempt.

"We'll get her," she growled at Torbon before storming off.

She had to believe it.

CHAPTER FIFTEEN

Back in the tunnels, the crew was quiet, and Taj understood. After what they'd witnessed, she couldn't blame them. There was nothing to be said after a display like that, people they'd known all their lives being executed in front of them with no way to be saved that didn't result in more needless deaths.

Memories flittered through Taj's brain, and her stomach tightened into a hard knot, an ember of disgust burning inside, threatening to set her alight like dry tinder. She'd held herself in check as the aliens killed her people, but now, removed from the situation, her fury simmered.

Taj wanted more than to simply rescue her people, she wanted revenge; to see the captain on his knees before her, begging for his life. Her lips trembling, she swore she'd see the man dead if it was the last thing she did.

The cold chill of the tunnel barely touched her as she slunk through the darkness, grateful for the ability to see in the dark. The staleness of the air seemed to close in on her, threatening to choke her at every harsh breath she sucked in.

Thoughts swirled in her head, plans, ideas, schemes, a churning maelstrom of what ifs and what could be. None amounted to anything, but she pushed on, desperate to think of some way she could get to the barn and free her people unseen.

She even cast a prayer Rowl's way, though she knew the great goddess wouldn't reply, even *if* she was listening. Rowl was a capricious god, more likely to sow chaos and create havoc than answer prayers. She'd thumb her nose in the direction of those of her kind unwilling to do for themselves, but still, Taj had to try.

She'd never once had so much riding on her decisions. To have it now was maddening, and Taj struggled to keep her thoughts positive, productive, but it was like hoping to see a reflection in a puddle during the rain. Everything was distorted, blurred beyond her comprehension.

"I need to get Jadie," Torbon mumbled, stumbling behind, putting distance between him and the rest of the crew as if he were ready to bolt away.

They stopped and turned to face him. While Cabe and Lina advanced on Torbon, closing the distance, Taj held her ground, wondering if it were better to let him go. They were all staring down the barrels of the enemies' guns, so would facing them head on be any worse than skulking about, trying to take the aliens out one at a time? Eventually, no matter what they did, things would escalate.

Still, when that time came, they had to be ready. Taj had to make them ready.

"We'll get her," Cabe assured, but there was no conviction in his voice. He was as lost and worried as the rest of them, adrift.

"We will," Lina reinforced as Torbon stared between them, no faith reflected in his eyes.

He stood limp, defeated, and it showed in the lines in his face and the slump of his shoulders. As much as he clearly wanted to believe in his crew, his friends, he couldn't.

"Hey," Taj said, inching forward to put a hand on his shoulder. "I know nothing we say matters right now, but like when I wanted to race up top and kill those soldiers for what they did to Beaux, I'm grateful all of you stopped me. It was stupid, an emotional outburst that would have cost me my life, and likely a whole bunch of others. The aliens would have seen the hatch and realized the tunnels are here. But you didn't let me. What was it you told me then?"

Torbon shrugged, his teeth gleaming as his upper lip peeled back in a tremble. He remembered well enough, but he simply didn't want to admit it since it didn't serve his cause then.

"You told me he was dead, that Mama needed us more, and—"

"I also said I needed to find Jadie," he interrupted. "I still feel that needs to be a priority. I should be out there—"

"I know," she told him, easing in closer, "but you also understood we had bigger things to worry about then. We still do, horrible as that is to say." Taj sighed, pushing on, even though she felt as if she were arguing the wrong side of the argument. "We need to rescue Jadie like we need to rescue everyone else, but we can't do that by hurling ourselves at the enemy as if we can take them head on. We can't, plain and simple, even with as much as we want to."

Taj hated to admit that, but she knew it was true. They had no more windriders to throw at the aliens, no way to even the odds. "We have to trick them, set traps, and lure them out into the open so we can whittle their numbers down to a manageable level. Then we can contemplate a real assault."

"And if we can't cut them down and weaken them?" Torbon asked.

Taj swallowed, letting the knot in her throat sink far enough for her to get her answer out. "Then we go down fighting."

Torbon sniffed. "They're gonna kill her, Taj!"

She nodded. "Given the chance, they'll kill all of us." She waved a hand over her head, in the general direction of the town. "There's no way that captain is gonna let any of us live, Torbon. We're in his way. He wants to claim them firing on us was some miscommunication, some protective instinct by his men."

Taj shook her head. "The reality is, they want something here badly enough to march out in force and take it, no matter who is in their way. They aren't going to simply take what they want and leave us be. Whatever it is they found, it's important to them. Important enough to kill us for it to keep us from interfering with their plans."

She grabbed Torbon under the chin and made him meet her eyes as a thought struck her, a way to say what she was trying to get across. "Right now, we, the free Furlorians, the ones they can't control, have the leverage."

"Yeah, right! How do you figure that?"

"We do," she argued. "Think about it." He clearly didn't look willing to, so she laid it out for him. In reality, she wanted to say what she was thinking and see if it sounded as crazy out loud as it did inside her head. "As long as we hold fast and keep interfering in their plans, our people have value to the enemy. They will keep them alive in order to try and lure us out of hiding."

"They'll keep killing them, too."

Taj nodded. "You're right, but only one or two if—"

"And that makes it all right?" Cabe asked, jumping in.

"No, of course it doesn't." She shook her head. "That's not what I'm saying, but you have to understand. This is much like what Beaux and Mama went through when they fled Felinus 4. People died because of the choices they made. It was never something they were proud of, or something they liked doing, but it was something they felt they *had* to do. People died for their choices. And like then, a few lives, however hurtful the losses might be, are better than all of us dying."

"You saying you're willing to die to get the rest out? You're willing to sacrifice all of us, too?" Torbon asked.

Taj drew in a slow, deep breath, giving herself a moment to answer. At long last, she gave a curt nod. "I am, Torbon," she told him. "If it means Jadie and the others get to live, get to survive and go on with their lives, then yes, I *am* willing to die. I'm also willing to risk all your lives—" she glanced at each in turn, lingering a moment on Cabe before ending on Torbon "—if doing so ensures our people survive. It's what Beaux and Mama would do. It's what's right."

Torbon sighed. "You and I have a different definition of *right*, too."

"Probably. But at the end of the day, I'll do whatever is necessary to rescue our people and see them safe. It's probably something I'll die for, and if I don't, it will be something even worse. It'll be something I'll have to live with." She sighed. "Trust me, this isn't something I'm deciding lightly. It isn't some heroic gack to make you or me feel better about all this."

"Good, because if it was, you suck at it," Lina said, shaking her head. "I'm still not sure I agree with any of this. It all sounds so crazy, so stupid."

Cabe stepped forward, his chest puffed out. "I know I'm gonna regret this, seeing how I agree with Lina, but I'm in. We need to do something."

"Me, too, I guess," Lina agreed, offering a crooked smirk that didn't inspire much faith in her commitment. "Not like we're spoiled with choices."

At last, after several moments of silence, all eyes on him, Torbon nodded. "I'm in if it means we rescue Jadie. I'll do anything to get her away from these sadistic freaks." He stumbled back and dropped to his butt, the wall against his back, signaling his acquiescence, however reluctantly.

Taj mustered a half-grin, offering it to each of them in hopes of gaining their confidence.

"So, what's the plan?" Cabe asked. "I mean, there has to be something bouncing around inside that skull of yours, right?"

That's an understatement, she thought. The problem was, she had too much bouncing around in her head to make much sense of it all. She had a skeleton of an idea, a direction to head in, but there was no plan, no concrete course of action.

"Well, since we know they are holding our people as bait to draw us to them in hopes of capturing or killing us all, we have to avoid doing that." Torbon started to argue, but Taj silenced him with a wave of her hand. "I'm not saying we don't try, but we have to be smart about it. We can't just storm the place or try to sneak in. They're expecting us, expecting that, and there's no way we'll make it work. We have to do something they aren't expecting."

"Then what do you propose?" Lina put her hands on her hips, ears wiggling with impatience.

"We need to scout the area better, to see if there is some opening we can exploit, some way in they haven't thought of."

"And if there isn't?" Lina pressed.

"We figure out what we're up against, and then we make an opening and go from there."

Cabe grunted. "You know, you make this all sound so nice and neat, like we have some secret weapon we can deploy against them when the time is right."

She shook her head. "I'm not trying to make it sound easy," she answered. "I know we don't have much in our favor. The two freighters we have access to are hidden in the sand bunkers out of reach, not that they'd do us much good against a destroyer; not even a grounded one. And I know we don't have a ton of weapons or people to confront these aliens. But all that works in our favor."

"We're smaller, weaker, outnumbered and outgunned, and yet that's a checkmark in the positive column?" Torbon said.

"Not when you say it like that, Torbon," she replied, sighing. "No, what I mean is, we know this town, we know the tunnels, and we know the surrounding area. We've all played and worked in it our whole lives. Between the four of us, we know every place to hide, every ferion spider pit, every trrilac mating route, and every watering hole there is for kilometers around."

"How does that help us?" Torbon asked.

"It helps us because we can plot and plan and lure them into traps as they give chase. Plus, it helps keep us alive longer."

"You thinking we can aim a trrilac herd this way or something?" Torbon asked.

She shrugged. "Maybe, but that wasn't exactly what I was thinking. Mainly, we need to figure out what it is they want from Krawlas. We need to know what's keeping them here, besides a damaged ship, and make sure we screw up their operations every step of the way."

"And if we make enough of a nuisance of ourselves, why won't they kill everyone to teach us a lesson?"

"Because then we have even more of a reason to keep doing what we're doing, Torbon. Think about it," she started. "If we disrupt their plans, and they kill all our people, they lose what little leverage they have."

"I thought you said they were leverage for us?" Lina raised an eyebrow, whiskers wiggling.

Cabe laughed. "I'm starting to think you've got a secret stash of nip you're holding out on."

"Leverage works both ways," Taj admitted. "As long as our people are alive, there's a chance we will give in to the pressure. And if we encourage that train of thought, let the aliens think we are being worn down by the threat to our people, then maybe we can accomplish our mission before they realize they don't hold the upper hand."

"But they do," Torbon told her, throwing his hands in the air. "They have Jadie. They have almost *everyone*!"

"But they *don't* have everyone," she replied, "and that's their problem. They have to weigh the value of their captives against what they'll lose if they kill them all."

"So, how do we convince them it's better to keep them alive while we do whatever it is we're gonna do?" Torbon asked.

"That brings us back to the plan," she countered. "We scout the area, see what we're facing in detail, not abstract, and examine everything. Then we make a decision based on that knowledge. Right now, we're guessing at every-thing, making presumptions we can't be certain are correct. We need to know more about our enemy, more about what they want from us, how important it is, and how we can minimize its value to buy time. Until we do all that, we're peeing into a sparkstorm."

"Fine!" Torbon said, almost spitting the word out. "How do you propose we start?"

"Not *we*; me," she answered. "You three stay down here and take care of Mama and get the people ready for what-ever happens, but don't let them know our plans."

Torbon chuckled. "Like we know what they are."

Taj shrugged. "The vaguer we are, the better, I think. We know the aliens have our people, and they have to be asking them about the rest of us, about—"

"You mean torturing them for our whereabouts, right?" Torbon sneered as he asked the question.

Taj swallowed hard and nodded. "Probably, and that makes all this only more important. We have to do whatever it is we're gonna do quickly because we have no idea if, or when, someone is gonna give up the tunnels. As soon as that happens, we're all dead, and anything we do is for naught."

"You really think someone would do that?" Lina asked. "Sell us all out?"

"If someone started ripping your claws out one by one, how long do you think you could keep your mouth shut?" Taj asked, eyes boring into hers.

Lina gulped.

"Exactly," Taj said. "The longer our people are held by the aliens, the more likely someone's gonna give in to the pain and tell them everything they know. When that time comes, we need to be packed up and gone."

"As if the destroyer's scanners won't notice half the town running away," Cabe argued.

"Which is why we need to be ready and do this right," she replied. "While I'm off scouting, you three need to round up the remaining Grans and elders. Figure out where we can safely relocate them before everything goes south on us. There's a greater chance they'll survive all this and recover once the aliens eventually leave if we can get the folks in the tunnels to scatter across the planet. We can sneak out of here in twos and threes, joining up once they are out of scanner range."

"So, we're back to running away?" Cabe asked.

"Not all of us, and you can think of it more as a tactical retreat in the best interest of our people. We convince some of the younger ones to stick around and fight alongside us, to help us even the odds a little. Otherwise, we get as many of the others out as possible," Taj told Cabe. "Ultimately, survival is our goal. The more of us who live on the better, right?"

It took a moment, but he finally offered up a reluctant nod.

She understood his hesitance. "Victory takes many forms, Cabe. It isn't always about a route or a crushed enemy lying dead on the battlefield. Sometimes, it's something as little as getting out alive, living to fight another day, but mostly just living. That thinking is what led our people to Krawlas, remember?"

He grunted. "And here we are, on the verge of extinction yet again. Seems our past tactics have worked out so well for us."

Taj let his point hang in the air, the stink of it making her nose twitch. She didn't want to give in to his pessimism, but she understood it. Sneaking around and fighting a guerilla war wasn't exactly what any of them had trained for.

It all seemed...cowardly, nothing at all like the brave heroics she'd grown up watching on the holos. What they were planning didn't feel like battle. It felt like murder, assassination. Yet, that was what the enemy had planned for them as a race.

She sighed. In the end, did it really matter how the enemy was defeated or how her people were saved? *No,* she thought, *it doesn't.* Victory, by whatever means, meant her people lived on.

If ever the ends justified the means, this was it.

"Stay here and prep our people to head out," she said at

last, breaking the oppressive silence that had settled over the group. "I'll be back soon, and we'll know better what to do then."

She started off without a glance back., By the time she reached one of the secret hatches leading out of the tunnels and up into the nearby desert, she'd even begun to believe they had a chance.

CHAPTER SIXTEEN

The trip back to town was exhausting.

Taj rubbed at her eyes and tapped herself on the forehead, fighting the natural decay of adrenaline. Up to now, she'd had some life or death situation to keep her veins firing, driving her on.

Out there in the dark, the quiet of night settled in over Culvert City, and the twin moons had slipped into the distance, taking their glowing orange light with them. Taj was beginning to feel the effects of the long, hard push to stay moving ever since they'd stumbled across the hostile alien forces, not even counting the trrilac catastrophe.

Over the course of the night, she'd slithered from shadow to shadow, rooftop to rooftop, and had, at long last, come to rest a few buildings away from the barns where her people were still being held. The guards around the perimeter were much the same in number as they had been the last time she'd been there, but there was a seriousness to their tone now; a deathly one.

Gone was the relaxed swagger of bored men who'd drawn the shortest straw duty of watching captives. Now, the men stood at rigid attention, their short, pacing steps crisp and attentive, heads on swivels as they held to formation and kept the barn under complete surveillance.

Taj bit back a groan. This was all because of her. She'd been the one to convince the crew to launch the *Thorn* at the shuttles, to escalate the fight. The aliens had been lackadaisical early on, thinking the Furlorians were no threat. But that was no longer.

Now, they were on their toes, not because she'd taken some of them out, but because she'd pissed off their captain with her stunt. His soldiers were paying for her attack, and she, in turn, had only made her job harder.

She thumped the side of her skull with a paw. *Idiot! What now?*

Keep doing what you're doing, you'll figure it out, she answered, smirking as she realized she was carrying on a conversation with herself.

"Now's not the time to go crazy, Taj," she whispered, shaking her head.

When better?

She chuckled, ignoring herself. Yes, her idea to wreck the shuttles might have been a bit impulsive given that she hadn't anything to follow the move up with, but she really couldn't regret it.

She'd made it harder for the enemy to flit back and forth between their ship and Culvert City. And if nothing else, she'd cost them some men and equipment. Anything she could do to frustrate and keep them from accomplishing their goal here was a good thing.

She stared out over the building, looking through the gazefinders, wishing she'd thought to bring one of the small radios that had been stored in the tunnels. While their signal was weak and limited in range, it would probably transmit beneath any frequency the aliens would use, so they probably wouldn't even know anyone was broadcasting.

And while there wasn't much to report, and the last thing she wanted to do was disappoint the crew given how much effort she'd put into getting them to agree with her, she could use a voice in her ear to keep her awake and aware.

Her head was heavy, and her mind was getting cloudy. Though she'd been knocked unconscious along the way, it was hardly anything considered rest. They'd been going nonstop ever since the trrilacs had been sighted. It was getting to her, frustration only adding to the weight that threatened to drag her eyelids closed.

Taj rubbed her eyes again, stifling a yawn, then slammed the gazefinders back against her face hard enough to elicit a quiet grunt. She surveilled the area again —*twenty-fifth time's the charm, huh?*—and fought against her drooping lids.

Then, as she convinced herself there was nothing to see and readied to give up and return to the tunnel, she caught a glimmer of motion at the barn nearest her. Soldiers were approaching it. She hunkered down lower in response, ignoring the puff of dust stirred up at her movement, and pressed the gazefinders to her face even harder.

There was a quiet knock, and the doors to the barn

eased open a few moments later, squealing the entire way. Voices drifted into the night.

"About time you relieved us," a soldier complained, stepping out where she could see him. Another trailed behind, slow and sluggish. Lights flickered behind them, but Taj couldn't tell see the source from where she crouched.

"Take that up with the captain," the man who had knocked answered. "He's got everyone working overtime on his little project out there, no exceptions. You've got about three hours of rack time before he drafts you, too." The soldier waved a hand toward the distance, and instinctively, Taj's gaze followed.

And for the first time, she realized there was a gathering out by the balboran pens she hadn't noticed before. She had been so focused on the nearby barn to see it.

Small lights gleamed near the pens, and she could barely make out the haze of movement, even with the magnification of the gazefinders glued to her face. The shuttle that had escaped her destructive trick hovered in the sky above the area. Its lights dimmed and angled in a direction that limited her ability to see it. The engines engaged only to hold it in place, she hadn't even heard them, amidst the constant chatter coming from the balborans.

Taj squinted, hoping to better see what was going on, but it did her little good. She could tell there was a congregation of machines and men there, but little to nothing else. Frustrated, she grunted and clambered over the side of the building. If she was going to get a better view, she would need to get closer.

She hit the ground with barely a tap of sound and shot off before she'd even settled her feet. The soldiers continued their conversation as she skirted the back edge of the nearest barn, staying out of the line of sight of the soldiers surrounding the next one over where her people were being held.

"I can't believe we're going to have to play in the dirt after sitting here all day," the soldier from the barn mumbled. His partner shook his head in obvious agreement.

"Be grateful for this duty," the other told him. "Most of the guys are being made to pull Vort's pet project for twenty hours straight, starting immediately. No one's going to get any rest until the captain's happy. You know that."

The first soldier grunted. "Happy? That'll never happen." All the men chuckled, but they kept their voices low, glancing around them as they did.

Taj grinned at their skittishness, thinking of ways it could be used against them. While the aliens were quick to follow their captain's orders, it was clear it was out of fear not loyalty.

It was something she had to think about, but Taj was sure that if she could twist the men against their commander, she could take advantage of the situation. She just needed to figure out how.

Right then wasn't the moment, however. She had a job to do so she filed that information away and crept closer to the soldiers, inching along the side of the barn and watching her every footfall to ensure she made no sound that would attract them.

The men clamored on for a few more minutes about nothing in particular, but Taj understood they weren't stationed in an abandoned barn for nothing.

Maybe they are backup for the other soldiers, she thought, a trap within a trap should Taj and her people find a way into the other barn.

And while that made sense, she couldn't help but wonder why there were only two soldiers there. If they wanted a substantive response to something happening, what good would two men do? As she contemplated their reasoning for such a small reactionary force, Taj heard something that chilled the blood in her veins.

"Scanners pick up anything?" the relieving soldier asked.

The other grunted. "Not a damn thing, not that I expected them to. With all the animal and troop movement nearby, the scanners are damn near useless this close to all that interference. We'd know if the locals came at us en masse, but there's no real way to determine if one or two are creeping up on us."

"So, you're saying they could be out there right now?" The men shuffled, the conversation dropping off a cliff into silence.

Taj stiffened and sunk deeper into the shadows. Her hackles rose, trailing uncomfortably down her back, and she fought to keep her tail from poofing. Had she made a noise or done something to clue them in to her presence?

Then the men laughed. "Yeah, like those cowardly rats are creeping around in the dark with some great escape plan in mind. The captain is delusional if he thinks the locals are plotting something. They're halfway across the planet by now, licking their wounds."

The soldiers continued to laugh. "Yeah, no doubt," one muttered. "Still, best not piss the captain off. We're going to hit the rack while you two assume scanner duties. Guess we'll see you in the morning."

There were some mumbled goodbyes and jibes, then the sound of weary footsteps stomping away. Taj waited a couple of heartbeats to make sure the soldiers were walking away from her location, then she shot off down the side of the barn.

When she reached the corner, she cast a furtive glance around the corner to see the two relieved soldiers disappearing down the street. The other two had gone inside the barn, and one of them was closing the door.

Opportunity slipping away, Taj bolted toward the barn door, hoping the squeal of its hinges would cover any noise she made. Fortunately, it did just that.

She pressed her back against the barn wall right where the hinges were attached and peeked in through the narrowing crack. What she saw stilled her heart in her chest, freezing it in place.

The image of dark steel and muted lights was burned onto her retinas, and her mind danced as it corroborated the shape and design with what she unconsciously knew the shape to be. Her heart fluttered back to life.

In the barn was the damaged shuttle they'd knocked over with the *Thorn*. It sat in relative silence, its wounds becoming visible in Taj's mind's eye even though the barn door was now fully shut, blocking her view.

That was why they only needed two men. It didn't take

more than that to operate or keep track of the ship's sensors on a full-time basis. They weren't there to assist the trap, they *were* the trap.

Were Taj and the others to sneak up on the barn in an effort to free their people, the shuttles scanners would pick them up and give the enemy real-time positioning and a tactical advantage the crew couldn't overcome.

And even though the soldiers had admitted the scanners were weak—distorted by the surrounding *noise* because they were meant for the wilds of open space and not the confines of a city—she knew well enough there was no way she or the others could sneak up on the barn in ones or twos and accomplish anything. It seemed the enemy knew it, too, or at least their commander did if the soldiers weren't so clued in.

Taj sighed and felt her fangs biting into her lower lip. Again, the enemy's tactical experience had thrown a wrench in the gears of her hopes, and once more, she felt the guilt washing over.

They wouldn't have gone to these lengths if she hadn't sicced the *Thorn* on them without a follow up plan. Unfortunately, there was nothing she could do about that now.

Her breath held tight, she slipped back the way she'd come. There were simply too many soldiers between her and the commotion she'd spotted near the pens, and she didn't think she could make her way closer without being seen, even if the shuttle scanners couldn't pick her up.

Her chest tight and with the sound of her heartbeat thundering in her ears, she made her way back toward the tunnel entrance. She was too tired to keep sneaking around, and she felt defeated on top of it all.

The aliens had countered her every plan before they'd even fully formed, and Taj couldn't keep her head on straight enough to think her way out of the labyrinth of things piling up against her and her people. She needed sleep, a little bit of a break to get her head and heart in order.

Too bad she wouldn't get it.

While she crept through the waning darkness, dawn on its way as she slipped into the desert, Lina bolted from the dunes and ran up to her. Taj didn't need to see the wrinkled lines of her face or the glistening of her eyes to know something was wrong. She could see it in the engineer's posture and in the quiet, shuddering sobs she fought to withhold.

"What is it?" Taj asked, really not wanting to hear the answer., She knew it would only bring more grief to her world.

And she was right.

"It's Mama. She's dying," Lina managed to sputter. "She's asking for you."

CHAPTER SEVENTEEN

Captain Vort drew in a deep breath, the coppery scent of blood filling his nose and setting it to tingling. He grinned, savoring the scent and staring down at the wreckage of the Furlorian his torturer, Kabal, left wriggling in the chair. Blood pooled around the captive, the puddle growing ever larger by the moment as the captive's movement slowed and faded.

"How much longer does he have?" Vort asked.

Kabal shrugged his lanky shoulders. "A minute, maybe two if I stanch some of the blood flow and patch the wounds. Hard to tell with these Furlorians, though. They're a hardy breed, despite their diminutive stature."

The captain waved the suggestion off. "Has it told you anything useful?"

The torturer shook his head. "No, and I don't believe it will. This one in particular is a stubborn beast, much the same as the others."

The captain stared at the torturer a moment, assessing

the man and his answer, finding both distasteful. Kabal was an abomination of a Wyyvan, which is what led Vort to believe it was why the man had chosen his profession to begin with. It seemed to fit him.

Tall and thin, easily looming a half-meter or more above Vort's height, Kabal was stringy muscle welded onto a scarecrow's frame. Thick green scars drew across his face and body, as though it were art and he the canvas.

Vort wondered how the man managed to even lift some of the heavier tools of his trade or how he was so successful at restraining his subjects, yet he always made do. He wore a leather apron and thick gloves, all of which glistened with the life of those who'd crossed the torturer's path.

Today, the stains were Furlorian blood and viscera, and much of it dripped from the treated leather as if it were rain off a tarp. Red dots spotted Kabal's face and upper chest, running like rivers through the stringy lines of muscle before dripping away.

Vort peeled his gaze from the torturer and walked over and seized the creature's chin, lifting it so they were eye to eye. Kabal drew back, out of his way. "Where are the rest of your people? Tell me, and I'll spare what's left of your life."

The Furlorian gurgled, crimson sputtering from its mouth and trailing down its furred chin, but there were no words mixed in. Its eyes rolled in its sockets, little more than brown dots in a sea of veiny red. Vort could tell it struggled to focus on him. There was nothing behind its empty stare. He sighed.

"This one is clearly broken beyond repair. You did your work too well, Torturer." Vort stepped back, allowing

Kabal to return to his post. "End it and bring out another. One of them must give up what we need eventually."

"Perhaps," Kabal said, whipping out a long-bladed knife and drawing a line across the Furlorian's neck.

The creature gasped, its voice turning into a wet, bubbling sound as it twitched against its restraints. Then, not more than a moment later, its chin dropped to its chest, blood gurgling from its wound like a broken fountain.

"But not all creatures warm to the knife."

"Or perhaps it's because this one was captured early and doesn't know where its brethren secreted themselves away. It might simply know nothing to tell us, as it might have been with the others laid fleshless in your domain."

Kabal conceded to the captain's logic with a nod.

"Pull one from the latest group captured. Maybe we'll have better results."

"Of course." Kabal waved to his assistant, and the man unshackled the corpse from the chair and dragged the body out of the room to dispose of it. "We will start immediately, Captain."

"Good," Vort replied. "Cut them all up if need be, Torturer, and let me know the moment you learn anything. We need to quell this malignant defiance before it takes root and spreads."

Kabal bowed at the waist, turning back to his tools and wiping the blood from his blade. Vort swallowed his disappointment and left the room, following in the trail of blood left by the dead Furlorian that had been dragged away. He made it a short way down the hall when Commander Dard caught up to him.

"Sir!"

"What is it, Commander?" Vort asked, not even bothering to slow. He had no more room in his head for disappointments.

"Sir, the amount of Toradium-42 on this planet is even more substantial than I'd first suspected."

That brought the captain up short. He turned to stare at Dard, one eyebrow raised. "Is it now?"

"Much more so." Dard nodded. "We've harvested twelve metric tons of Toradium-42 already, and that's mostly from scraping the surface. We've the shuttle ferrying as much of the mineral as it can haul back to the *Monger* as we speak."

The captain grinned, unable to restrain the mirth building inside him despite realizing they could have hauled so much more had the other shuttles not been laid low.

He leaned in close to Dard, though he was certain there was no one near enough to hear their conversation. "Be sure to stockpile a reasonable, personal cache of the mineral, should our efforts for the empire not be as...*commensurate* as befitting our efforts, Commander." He cast another furtive glance about. "I would hate for our achievements here to be *mistakenly* overlooked by Command."

"Indeed, Captain," Dard agreed. "That would be most...unfortunate."

"That it would." Vort offered his second a broad grin and went to walk away, only then realizing the commander had held his ground. "Is there anything else, Commander?"

Dard nodded. "The men have detected a rich vein

running under the pens of those strange creatures the locals call balborans. The vein runs deep. It's cluttered and would nearly double their current excavation within the same time frame. They are asking permission to mine it."

"Would it now?" Vort sucked in a deep breath and let the thought bounce about inside his skull. "Tell them they have the go ahead, but I don't want the animals slaughtered or set free. They might be useful should we run low on supplies before Command sends a crew to replace us. No point in wasting resources given we have no idea how long we'll be on this forsaken, backwater planet."

"Understood, sir."

"Have the men herd the creatures into one of the other nearby pens. We might well lose a few to overcrowding, but I'd rather have the mass of the beasts available should we be forced to search for alternate food sources. I'd rather not have to hunt the creatures down should our circumstances become difficult."

"I'll pass the order along, Captain."

Vort patted the man on his shoulder. "We've come far together, Commander. Once Command sees the hoard we've amassed here, I can see us traveling much farther. Politics maybe?"

Dard chuckled and conceded with a quick nod. "That is something I would like to see, Senator Vort."

The captain smiled. "The title has a pleasant ring to it, does it not?"

"It does indeed, sir."

"Then let us be certain nothing stands in our way, Commander." He gave the man's shoulder a squeeze and started off down the hallway.

Despite the unfortunate circumstances that had befallen the mission—the failed efforts to corral the local population, as well as the disappointing situation with the shuttles—Vort felt confident he had headed off further incidents with his demonstration in town and his redistribution of his assets. He needed only to concentrate on mining the planet dry of Toradium-42 and fending off the occasional desperate guerilla assault upon his soldiers.

And that was only if his torturer failed him, and for all the things Kabal was guilty of, failure was never one of them. He would ferret out the hiding places of the local rats, and Vort would rain fire down upon them. It was only a matter of time.

Soon, he could turn his back on Command and Grand Admiral Galforin once and for all.

The thought brought a smile to his face, and the captain made his way toward his cabin. Given his mood, a good, stout shot of Wyyvan Valmuth Rum would be the perfect end to the day.

Maybe two shots.

CHAPTER EIGHTEEN

Taj ran through the tunnels, kicking up dust and gasping to catch her breath. The tiredness of the last few hours was gone, burned away by an all-new adrenaline rush of terror ignited by the idea of losing Mama Merr.

No, not so soon after Beaux, she kept thinking, over and over again, the thought a thick mire filling her skull and making her ears ring. *It's* too *soon.*

Still, Lina had been adamant as to Mama's condition. She'd gone downhill since Taj had left her side, and there was no one around, no one left, to nurse her back to health.

Lina chattered the entire way, filling Taj's head with the horrible truth of it all: Mama was old and frail, belying the fierceness of her attitude. She'd survived far longer than anyone could have imagined, and there was simply no coming back from a broken spine at her age, and who knew what else had been injured that they were unable to diagnose.

Taj had known it was only a matter of time before she

heard someone tell her of Mama's passing, but she'd put it out of her mind, unwilling to even contemplate the possibility. Even now, she argued with herself, lying and telling herself that Mama would be fine, that the old queen would make it through this like she had everything else the universe had thrown at her over the course of her life.

But when Taj dropped to her knees beside the old Gran, she could no longer deny the direness of Mama's situation. It was written plainly in the trembling furrows that lined her face, the droop of her cheeks, her whiskers hanging like browning leaves after the first freeze.

Mama was dying.

Taj bit back a sob as she grabbed the old Gran's cold, trembling hand. It felt like ice. "I'm here, Mama. I'm here."

Mama Merr's eyes rolled to the side slowly, like fish swimming upstream, until they locked on Taj at long last. "Child," the old queen muttered, the word barely more than a ragged whisper.

"I'm here," Taj repeated, fighting to keep from repeating herself again, unsure of what else to say. "I-I—"

Mama squeezed her hand, and though Taj barely felt it, the effort drew her up short. She went silent, grateful for the reprieve that kept her from spewing the waterfall of thoughts and feelings that crowded her throat and battled her tongue in order to be spat out.

"We-we've little time, child," Mama told her, each word brittle. "Listen to me now li-like you never have before."

It took all of Taj's willpower to keep from blubbering. Instead, she gave a shallow nod of deference, letting the old queen speak her last words without interruption. And as Mama licked her lips and summoned the strength to speak,

Taj felt the tunnels shrink around her, the darkness creeping closer as her people rallied behind her, crowding in to listen.

Their breaths wafted warm over Taj, making her ears twitch and her tail to *thwap*. She tucked it in instinctively to keep it from being stepped on, but her gaze never left Mama's eyes. She encouraged her with a bitter smile, battling the sadness waiting to swoop down and carry her away.

"Our people will...will be yours to lead very soon, my child," she said, the sentiment mimicking what Beaux had told her before he sealed the hatch to his fate.

The words struck Taj like a physical blow, and she collapsed onto her tail, her legs trembling too hard to support her any longer. Both of her parents—as she could think of them as nothing other—dying so soon after one another was a wound she could feel being carved into her heart, one that would never fully mend.

Both wanted her to lead the last of their people. It was clearly something they had discussed at length among themselves without Taj's knowledge, and it was an honor she couldn't remotely begin to appreciate at that moment. Right then, the declaration was salt in that same, gaping wound.

"For now, y-you must help Gran Beaux do what...what must be done to stop this in-invasion, t-to help our people recover."

Taj bit her tongue to keep from telling Mama the truth, that the love of her life, Beaux, was dead, and Mama was on her way to meet him on the other side, Rowl willing.

Taj's tail stiffened, poofing at her dishonesty and

disgust with herself, and she was grateful then for the darkness that encroached, keeping the tell-tale sign of her lie from Mama. She'd never been able to lie to the old woman, and she lamented the fact that she had to now.

"I will," Taj managed to spit out, snapping her mouth shut right after to hold back anything else that might slip free.

Mama smiled and gave another squeeze of her hand. Taj could feel her strength oozing away. "See our people safe, child, and...and know, n-now and forever, you are...are loved."

With the last of her strength, Mama Merr pulled Taj's hand to her mouth and kissed it. Her final breath warmed the fur on the back of her paw, stirring it with its passage, and then there was nothing more but still, silent emptiness.

Taj crumpled onto Mama and let loose a howl that rattled her ribs, the tears and recriminations overwhelming her as though she herself had been the one to die. She barely heard the muffled sobs of those around her as the gravity of Mama's passing fell over her, a funerary shroud of cold black despair.

And then she heard nothing, caught up in the tsunami of sadness that washed the wreck of her away.

Many hours later, when at last Taj could draw a breath not tinged with tears, she had crept away from Mama's stiffening body that was now wrapped in cloth and laid in reverence for all to say their farewells. Taj found a quiet alcove away from the mass of traffic mourning their lost leader. The crew had followed Taj and, quite uncharacter-istically, held their silence as she struggled with her feelings.

She knew they, too, felt the loss as sharply as she did, hence their clustered quiet, but she couldn't think beyond herself right then. Too many people had died, and her head spun with it all. Guilty as she felt, she simply couldn't bring herself to commiserate with the others right then.

It was all too personal, too raw for her to reach out and offer them her support like she knew she should. It was too brittle, too weak to sustain herself, let alone the others. She had to see her way clear before she could see anything else.

A few hours must have passed since she'd crawled away. It was only when Grady wobbled up, clearing phlegm from his throat to get their attention that Taj lifted her head. It was only then that she could truly comprehend the sorrow of her friends.

She sniffed, as if waking for the first time in ages, and reached out to them. The crew entwined shaking fingers as the elder Tom stood patiently, leaning against the wall to keep from swaying too much. His pipe hung from parted lips, teeth gnawing at the stem. Taj caught a hint of nip in the still smoking embers.

Lina pressed her head onto Taj's shoulder, quiet whim-pers reverberating between them. Cabe inched in close and wrapped a long arm about them both, pulling them in tight. Torbon sat on the other side, giving them the tiniest bit of space, but Taj would have none of it.

She grabbed a handful of his fur, ignoring his sharp hiss, and pulled him into the others. She felt his resistance waver and fall away almost immediately, and she offered him the brightest smile she could muster.

It barely wiggled her lips, but when she saw him return it, his no more defined than her own, it set loose a soothing balm into her bloodstream, a sad peace settling over, a somber realization striking home.

For all Taj had lost that day, she still had so much.

"I'm sorry to bother you," Grady told them, the sour expression on his face telling them he was anything but sorry, "but much as I wish we weren't here mourning Merr, tragedy that it is, we ain't out the woods yet. We need to—"

"What the gack? You don't get to tell us what we—" Cabe shouted, pulling his legs beneath him, readying to pounce, but Taj tightened her grip on him and held him in place, heading off his outburst before it could fully erupt.

"No, Cabe," Taj cut in, "he's right." She clambered to her feet, reluctantly peeling away from her mourning crew, but keeping some part of her body touching each, her hand settling on Cabe's shoulder. "We don't have time for this, for fighting among ourselves."

"Bloody Rowl, Taj!" Cabe rose to his feet despite her restraining hand, his chest puffed out. "We just lost Mama, right after we lost Beaux. You can't expect us to run off and—"

Taj leaned in and planted a kiss right on Cabe's mouth, silencing him outright. He gasped and stumbled back, and Taj took the opportunity to continue.

"This is exactly the time our expectations should be the highest, Cabe," she told him, casting her gaze across the others and receiving a nod from old Grady. "Much as I want to crawl into a hole and cry until I drown myself, now is not the time for it. Our people," she glanced over at Torbon, "our *families*, are in danger. Whatever tears we have to shed can wait, but our families can't."

Cabe growled and punched the wall, kicking up a small cloud of dust. She could see his eyes gleaming through the haze, and though there was fury there, fires illuminating his brown eyes, she could see reason seeping in and taking hold.

He spit a mouthful of nip juice onto the floor and shook his head, but he went quiet, still, his defiance shifting to a sullen calm. She turned and gave Grady a thankful nod for his nudge, and the old Tom returned a careful smile and spun about, hobbling off without another word.

"What do you want to do," Lina asked.

"I already told you what I want," Taj answered, "but since I can't cry myself into oblivion and wish everything back to normal, we need to do more than that."

"What do you suggest." Torbon slunk against the wall, pulling Lina along with him. She gave in without complaint. The two cradled each other, narrow, tired eyes watching Taj. Cabe continued to stand rigid, but his gaze remained steady on the group.

"Honestly?" Taj asked. "I'm not really sure what to do yet, I'm so damn tired."

She looked at the others and saw the same expression on their faces that she imagined was plastered across her own: a bone-numbing weariness each fought to keep at bay. It was clearly a losing battle.

"We need to sleep, to rest and recharge, if only for a few hours." Taj gestured toward the tunnel ceiling. "The sun is well into the sky by now, and the aliens will be out and about, ready for us, waiting. We need the cover of darkness, shadows, if we're to succeed."

"And if they kill more of our people while we're asleep?" Torbon asked, and though he didn't mention her by name, it was clear he meant Jadie.

Taj swallowed the bile that rose into the back of her throat at the thought of him being right and gave herself a moment to let the bitterness drain away. "We've already discussed my thoughts on this, Torbon. And as much as I feel for what you're going through, we have to believe this Captain Vort will stay true to his word, at least until tonight's gathering."

Torbon snarled. "So, we're supposed to trust this piece of gackspit to keep his word?" His hackles rose, the fur about his neck thickening in menace.

Taj shook her head. "Trust? No, but he wants this over as quickly as we do," she said, jabbing a claw in Torbon's direction. "He gains nothing but resentment and more defiance if he goes against his word on this. No," she went on, "he needs us to surrender, to give in to him. Whatever he wants here has his full attention, or he wouldn't waste his time threatening. He doesn't want to have to deal with us, which is why he came in guns blazing right away. Vort planned to take us out from the start, and only our perseverance kept that from happening. He hadn't expected that."

"And now that we've become a thorn in his side, rest in peace, little windrider, he's not prepared to pull his efforts away from his true goal and chase after us," Cabe mumbled, clearly starting to wrap his head around what

Taj was getting at.

"He's not confident he can take us all out without it impacting his real purpose," Lina said.

"Exactly," Taj confirmed, rubbing at her temples, massaging her brain to keep her sluggish thoughts flowing. "As soon as he figures out where the rest of us are, which he's clearly having a hard time accomplishing, that's when you can expect he'll make a determined run at us. Until then, he's herding cats." She chuckled at her own joke, laughing until she'd dragged the others along.

"That was bad," Torbon told her, shaking his head after a few moments, catching his breath.

"Right?" Lina agreed. Cabe grinned in agreeance.

"Anyway," Taj started again once they'd caught their collective breath. "Right now, he's playing a waiting game, using our people against us, setting traps like he has at the barn because his focus is split."

"What's there?" Cabe asked. "You never did tell us what you saw."

"Yeah, it's been a little crazy since then," she admitted and felt herself starting to get dragged down again, but she shrugged the melancholy aside. "He's hidden the shuttle we knocked over in the southernmost barn, and he's got round-the-clock crews onboard, watching the scanners in case we mass up and try and free the prisoners."

"There's no way they can pick up one or two of us, though," Torbon said, his eyes lighting up. "Their scanners can't be that sensitive."

"They aren't," she agreed. "I overheard the men saying exactly that, and I'm certain it was just them running their mouths and letting the info slip, not some master plan of deception to lure us in a few at a time."

"We can use that!" Torbon went to jump to his feet, but Lina clung to him and held him down.

"We can, but later," Taj told him, reinforcing Lina's hold with a raised palm.

"Yeah, there are still a bunch of soldiers on watch there. While one or two of us could sneak over there and not be detected by the scanners, the men would see us, for sure," Cabe told them, clearly processing his thoughts aloud more so than actually joining the discussion. "Still, this is something we need to think on and see how it helps us, and what we can do with the information."

Torbon snarled, but he relented a moment later, sinking into Lina's grasp. "Yeah, I can see that being a problem. As long as the soldiers are outside the barn like they are, they'll shoot everyone in the back, even if we sneak people out a couple at a time. There are simply too many eyes out there now."

Taj nodded. "Especially since the last of their shuttles is patrolling nearby. It will spot us from the air even if the other's sensors don't."

"We need to take out both of the shuttles," Cabe suggested, "though I'm not sure how we'd manage that. We don't have much in the way of explosives. We could probably grab a couple of those grenades from the soldiers. I'm sure there are some lying about, but I doubt they'd even scratch the paint on those ships. They're meant for deep space and inter-atmospheric transport."

He sighed. "They're built sturdy. The only reason we managed to do so much damage with the *Thorn* was that the shuttles had their hatches open, allowing the extra fuel we strapped to the wings to get inside, past the armor to the more sensitive equipment."

"We need to steal one then," Torbon muttered, licking his lips.

"Good luck with that." Cabe grinned. "Same problem: no way to get inside the stupid thing unless we're there exactly when they change crews. Even then, we'll be outnumbered and outgunned. All the aliens have to do is yell to bring dozens more soldiers down on our heads since we can't go in more than two at a time. And even if we manage to get by all that, we're not even sure we can fly the damn things."

Torbon slumped against the wall, rubbing at his eye. "Rowl, but I hate this."

"We all do, Torbon," Taj told him.

"There has to be something we can do," Torbon moaned.

"I'm sure there is," she agreed, "but none of us are gonna think of it as worn out as we are. Like I said earlier, we need to sleep a little, let our heads settle, then maybe eat something. After that, we'll have the night draped over us again, our wits about us, and we can better put all the pieces of this puzzle together."

Cabe and Lina muttered their agreement, and even Torbon conceded after a while, slinking down even lower and pulling Lina tighter against him. He yawned loudly, almost comically, not even bothering to cover his mouth as his eyeteeth gleamed in the gloom.

"Yeah, let's sleep for a bit," he said. "Jadie will be okay

for now." Without another word, his chin slumped, and quiet snores sputtered out.

Lina was out next, with Cabe coming over and settling in beside Taj before passing out a moment later. Taj sighed, thoughts of Beaux and Mama nipping at her, and rested her head against Cabe's cheek. There was no resisting the warmth and comfort any longer.

She fell asleep to the lullaby of his twitching whiskers tickling her eyelids.

CHAPTER NINETEEN

The world swayed and danced, a great rumble echoing through the shallow tunnel of awareness that had begun to creep past Taj's unconsciousness. She clasped at the cold floor and felt her claws scrape against stone.

Cabe gasped somewhere in the gloom, and Taj's eyes fluttered as sleep was swept away. She bolted upright with a choked hiss as dream and reality collided, adrenaline setting her nerves alight.

"What the gack?" she muttered, blinking the sleep from her eyes. "You guys feel that?"

The question hung in the air unanswered as the world shimmied once more and she lost her balance, stumbling into the wall. The impact knocked the last of her weariness from her, and she growled, her vision drawing into focus.

She saw Cabe, not more than a meter from her, scrambling to his feet, eyes wide and uncertain. Lina was nearby. She clung to the wall as dust glittered like stars in the early morning dawn of the tunnel. Then a bustle of footsteps snatched her attention from her friends. A small queen, barely half Taj's height, careened into the room, feet slipping across the stone.

"The aliens have broken into the tunnels! They've found us!"

Taj clasped her heart. It felt as if it exploded, spattering her ribs with ragged chunks of terror. "They what?" It was if the words wouldn't come together in any coherent order in her head, even though she'd heard the little cat clearly.

Fortunately, Lina had more of her wits about her than Taj.

"Where?" the engineer asked.

"Northeast corner, up around the pens."

Taj stiffened. *Right where I saw them last night,* she remembered. Her thoughts whirled, though the more she thought about it, the less it seemed to make sense. There wasn't a hatch up that way. *Then how could they—*

"Gather our people near the desert exit," she told the little cat, brushing the thought away. It would do her no good to speculate. "Get them ready to run if the aliens get past us." She checked to make sure her bolt pistol was still secure in her holster and bolted off down the tunnel, calling back to her crew. "Come on!"

The others followed an instant later, and Taj let out a grim *mrowl,* her imagination stoking the embers of her fear. She'd known it was only a matter of time until the aliens found their way into the tunnels, but she hadn't been ready for it.

From the start, despite knowing her fellow Furlorians were being tortured, she'd hoped and prayed the alien invaders would never find their way to the secret hideout under the earth, but that hope had been shattered.

She ran on, footsteps pattering down the long corridors. As far as she was from the location where the aliens had supposedly broken into the tunnels, there was no way they could hear her yet, so she ran on without hesitation, clasping her pistol. The closer she came, the more her heart drummed a dirge against her ribs.

She hadn't given much thought to what she and the others were doing when she'd first started off, but as she neared her objective, realization had sunk home like a feral kitten's teeth. She was running to her death, dragging her crew right along with her.

Taj gasped and nearly stumbled, catching her balance at the last moment.

If the aliens had found them, they would be swarming the secretive tunnels in force, an army there to root out the remaining Furlorians with prejudice. What hope did she and her crew have of repelling a full-on assault by the invaders?

None.

The answer dripped uninvited into her brain.

By then, though, it was too late to alter their course. Taj caught a whiff of scorched earth and the musky scent of the balborans pens. She skittered to a stop, whiskers flickering as she tightened her grip on her gun.

She raised a fist to stop her crew behind her. They came to a muffled halt at her back without a word, and Taj heard voices echoing through the tunnel ahead: strange, alien voices, distorted by their armored visors.

"Loz, damn it!" the first voice shouted.

"You all right?" another asked, the second voice seeming to come from a greater distance.

"Yeah, I think so."

"Stay there then," the second came back. "Give us a minute to get some rope."

Taj stiffened at hearing the voices, the conversation drifting in her head but not making any sense given what she'd pictured was happening.

She turned to her companions and pointed at the ground where they stood, imploring them to stay put. She needed to get closer to see what was going on, but Taj didn't want to risk the lives of her crew any more than she already had. Besides, if her suspicions were right, it was best they stay where they were anyway.

Without waiting for her crew to respond, she slunk off, covering her nose and mouth as dust and dirt swirled about, choking the corridor the closer she came to where the aliens had broken through.

A dim light broke through the collapsed ceiling a short distance ahead, drawing Taj in. She held her breath and crept closer, her back so close to the wall that she could feel its cold stone emanating through her fur.

The quiet shuffle of pacing footsteps wafted to her ears a moment later, and she caught snippets of incoherent muttering. She slowed even further, coming to a halt near a mound of debris that had collected on the near side of the tunnel break. It had gathered in the curve and providing cover for her approach. The muttering continued from the other side, scraping bootsteps punctuating every complaint.

"The captain's going to skin me," Taj heard an alien

mutter. "Get me out of here," he then called out, directing his ire toward someone invisible above.

A cold chill skittered down her spine at his words, realization sinking in to reinforce her earlier uncertainty. Now she understood why the conversation she'd heard hadn't made sense.

These aliens weren't storming the tunnels; they'd stumbled across them by accident.

Taj grinned. They hadn't discovered the Furlorians' hiding place. At least not yet.

"What's down there?" a voice called out from above.

"Shit if I know," the fallen alien replied. "It's a damned tunnel. We hit some kind of sinkhole or something."

Taj dared a glance around the corner to see the alien waving his arms at another, whose face appeared in the hole above, head surrounded by a halo of morning light. The helmeted alien hovered there for a moment in silence before started up again, his visored gaze shifting back and forth between his companion and the mouth of the tunnel where Taj lurked.

"We're getting rope to get you out, but you should do a little recon while you're down there." The alien jabbed a finger toward the tunnel. "The walls there don't look entirely natural."

Taj groaned under her breath. He was right. Though the Furlorians had found the tunnel system, they had worked over the years to expand and reinforce them and smooth the walls. And though the section they were in now had been the last of the labyrinth worked on, a close enough inspection of the stone would let anyone know there had been outside assistance for them to have reached their current state of functionality. Given who resided on the planet, it wouldn't take more than a second before the aliens realized the Furlorians were using the place to hide from the invaders.

"You want me to explore the damn place?" the trapped alien asked.

"Why not? You got something better to do?"

The first alien grumbled something quiet enough to not be clear, but Taj didn't need to understand it to know he was cursing the soldier above.

"Me and Frol will be down to help in a minute, as soon as we secure the rope, so take a quick peek ahead. Hopefully this is nothing, but with the captain on a rampage, I sure ain't going to give him an excuse and say we weren't thorough. How about you?"

The trapped alien grunted, setting the steam in his hoses to frothing. "All right already." He waved a hand, shaking his head, and started in Taj's direction. "I'm going but get that damn rope ready. I don't want to spend all day down here."

Taj bolted back down the tunnel as the soldier came her way. Fortunately, he took slow, measured steps, examining everything as he went. Taj ran into her crew, all of them chomping at the bit. She huddled in close.

"They don't know we're here," she whispered. "Not yet, at least, but there's a soldier headed our way, exploring the tunnels. Won't be long before he realizes this is where all our people disappeared to."

"What do we do?" Lina asked, visibly stiffening as the scrape of the alien soldier's boots sounded a little way down the corridor. The pistol in her hand trembled.

Taj drew in even closer. "We need to take him out quickly and quietly," she said. "There'll be a couple more following him in a a few minutes."

"We can't let them hear us then," Cabe insisted, drawing a nod of agreement from the others.

He broke away from the huddle and glanced around the tunnel. Taj saw what he did, realizing there was little cover for them to hide behind with only one small alcove nearby. He waved the crew toward it as the thump of bootsteps drew closer. Taj shook her head and ushered the others into the alcove, remaining outside.

"What are you doing?" Lina hissed?

"Being bait," she answered, and there wasn't time to say anything else.

The soldier came around the bend in the tunnel and spotted her. Taj slipped her weapon from view, stuffing it into the belt of her uniform at the base of her back, and she dropped to her knees with a sob.

"Please, don't hurt me," she cried.

"What the—?" the alien asked, his surprise obvious even through his visor. The steam in his breathing apparatus gurgled. "Stay where you are!" he shouted, raising his rifle and starting forward. "Don't you move."

Taj offered a compliant nod, sniffling. Though everything was going according to plan—if it could be called a plan at all—she didn't have to fake her fear.

She knew gack well that Captain Vort wanted her and her people dead. There was nothing keeping her alive but the hope that this soldier wanted to capture the captain's good graces by bringing him a prisoner who knew where the rest of the Furlorians were squirreled away.

Inch by inch, he drew closer, gun raised, ready to tap the trigger and end Taj's last-minute ruse of servility. "Please," she said again. "Don't kill me." Taj sunk deeper, groveling against the stone flooring.

"I should," the alien answered, but she could see his confidence growing. What menace was there in a single, small Furlorian anyway?

Taj buried a grin behind her cowed head. He'd find out shortly.

She raised her hands and scuttered backward.

"Stay where you are, or I'll—"

He didn't get more than that out before a furred blur crashed into him and slammed him into the nearby wall.

There was a sharp *crack* as the alien's visor shattered against the stone. The soldier grunted, shaking his head to clear it, but Cabe didn't relent. He pinned the alien against the wall and kicked his legs out from under him. The alien hit the floor with a curse, struggling to bring his rifle around, but that never happened.

Taj shot forward and pushed her hand inside the alien's helmet, through the broken visor. Her claws found his eyes and sunk in. The soldier gasped, the sound quickly turning into a ragged shriek. Taj hardened her will, steeling herself for what she needed to do, and tightened her grip. Then she yanked her hand from the alien's helmet, raking her claws across his eyes, tearing one out.

She felt blood pulse, warm and wet, in her palm. She cast the grisly trophy aside, stumbling into the wall at her back as the soldier thrashed about. She stared at him, the alien clawing at his wound as though he could stop the gusher of blood spilling free from his face and filling his helmet. Her stomach churned at what she'd done, how easy it had been to maim another creature, blinding him with her own bare hands.

She pressed her palm against the alien's chest, leaving a red handprint behind, while the soldier whimpered, going still as the pain overwhelmed him, and unconsciousness took hold.

The crew looked at her, eyes wide. It was one thing to fire back on an enemy, killing them before they did you, but what she'd done was up close and personal. It was the type of fighting Mama Merr had spoken about. And Taj knew it would change her.

All of them did.

But before despair could sink its talons in deeper and force her into a fetal ball while she questioned her every action, more voices rumbled down the tunnel, coming from where the aliens had broken in. Taj shook her morbid thoughts clear and rolled the soldier over, her hands yanking at his gear despite the crews' confused stares.

There was still more to be done.

She pushed her disgust away and snatched one of the silver devices from the alien's belt.

"S'thlor!" a voice shouted in the near distance. "Where are you?"

Taj rose from the alien corpse, swallowing hard. "Bind his wounds and keep him alive," she whispered, then shot off toward the voices that grew louder with every second.

"What are you—?" Cabe started to mutter behind her, but she didn't stop to respond.

She continued down the corridor, not bothering to hide her presence. A moment later, she skittered around the last corner separating her from the other aliens who'd invaded their tunnels. She grinned when the pair spied her.

"Hey!" the first of the aliens called out. "What are you—?"

She answered his question with action instead of words. Taj twisted the device like she'd seen the soldiers do and tossed it their way. Both aliens went rigid at the sight. There was a moment of silence, the only sound in the tunnel the metallic clank of the grenade bouncing across the floor. The men finally gathered their wits, screamed, and spun about before bolting.

"Run before—"

Taj had done just that. She darted around the corner, putting the stone wall between her and the grenade. The aliens had no such protection.

There was a horrendous *boom*, and the tunnels swayed drunkenly under Taj's feet. She crashed into her crew, taking them to the ground with her in a heap of tangled limps and hissed curses.

Dust spilled from the ceiling, coating them in a cloud of gray. A deep, rumbling echo filled their ears as the cavern collapsed behind them, burying the alien soldiers under ton of rubble and debris.

And as much as Taj hated that she was responsible for their deaths, a quick glimmer of Mama Merr washed over her, and Taj couldn't help but grin. While these particular soldiers might not have been directly responsible for the old Gran's death, there was a satisfying irony in the way they'd been killed, the roof coming down on top of them as it had Mama.

Taj sighed and disentangled herself from her crew,

inching over and pressing her back to the wall. Their wide eyes followed her, cautious expressions defying the curiosity she knew they felt. She ignored their unspoken questions and gestured toward the alien on the floor.

"He still alive?"

Lina nodded. "Barely."

"Good." Taj clambered to her feet. "Then let's grab him and get back to our people."

"What do you want with this guy?" Cabe asked, going over to scoop the soldier up despite his obvious reticence.

"He might be useful," Taj answered, moving to help Cabe. "He knows things that might be important to us."

"So, you plan to torture him," Lina asked, "like they're doing to our people?"

Taj shrugged. "Time is running short, and they're not leaving us much in the way of options," she answered with a sigh. "I don't want to do this any more than you do, but if it helps our people get out of this safely, then I'll do whatever I need to." She met the engineer's gaze until Lina relented and looked away.

It's what Mama and Beaux would do.

Together, the crew carried the wounded soldier through the tunnels, and Taj pushed aside any thoughts of right and wrong. She could worry about that later. Right now, it was all about making sure her people were safe.

They'd gotten lucky the aliens had only stumbled across the tunnels by accident, a byproduct of whatever it was they were doing. They wouldn't be so lucky next time, and anything Taj could do to prepare her crew and people for the next attack, she would do it.

Including torturing an alien soldier.

She drew in a slow, deep breath, and held it until it soured in her lungs before letting it slip loose. This wasn't who she wanted to become, but she couldn't see any other way. Besides, if all she had to sacrifice to keep her people safe was her innocence, it was worth it.

At least she hoped it was.

CHAPTER TWENTY

It took the crew nearly a half hour to get the wounded alien back to where the others were gathered. Lina had run ahead to let everyone know they were safe, and that they didn't have to run. Not yet, at least.

A small group of Furlorians met the crew at a small chamber cut off the side of the tunnels. That's where Taj and Cabe dumped the soldier. Grady stood there alongside Gran Em, both of them rubbing at their paws.

Taj knew the look. It was one of dissatisfaction. She didn't let it stop her, though, and she ignored the narrow glares of the pair.

Snubbed, Gran Em cleared her throat. "Why did you bring that *thing* here?" she asked.

"He might be able to tell us more about the enemy," Taj answered without so much as looking back at the Gran.

"And you think he'll simply divulge that information to you?"

Taj stiffened and turned on a heel to face the old Gran.

"I don't expect anything except that I'm going to do my best to find out whatever I can to help us."

She told Cabe to stay put, then waved Lina off after some water for their prisoner. Though she figured it would come down to her torturing the alien for information, she wanted to try a different tact first. If she could avoid bloodying her hands, that'd be the best route. But if she had to...

That thought trailing off inside her head, the alien groaned, and Cabe settled him upright with his back against the wall. They'd stripped him of his weaponry and communication devices on the trip through the tunnels, not that he had much. Taj made sure Cabe stayed nearby so the alien didn't get a chance to do something unexpected.

The soldier stared at Taj with bloody sockets, swollen shut. He said nothing, simply licking his lips and waiting. Taj pushed a flask of water against those same lips once Lina returned, doing her best not to stare at the wreckage of his features.

"Here, take a drink."

The soldier complied, gulping down several sips before Taj pulled the flask away. "That's enough for now. I'll give you more in a moment," she told him.

"Will you?" he asked, his voice jagged and raw.

Taj nodded, then muttered a quiet, "Yes," realizing the alien couldn't see her. *You blinded him,* the thought rang out, and she shook her head to push it aside. She couldn't think about that right then. For all that had happened, she'd been fighting for her life.

She still was, for that matter.

"Look, I need to ask you some questions, and if you

decide not to answer them, I'll be forced to hurt you further," she said. "Do you understand?"

He nodded without hesitation. "I'm dead already, Furlorian. There's no coming back from this with my people." He gestured to his face, then to the tunnels surrounding him in a general manner. "I'm a lost cause now."

"What do you mean?" Taj heard Grady and Em shuffle closer, grabbing a spot alongside the crew.

"Captain Vort has no use for a blind, captured soldier," he replied. "Were he to know I was here, he would kill me right alongside all of you without any hesitation." He shrugged again. "Better I take my chances with you and plead for mercy than hope my *precious* captain will take pity on me." He said the last with phlegmy chuckle.

Despite herself, Taj grinned. She'd known the aliens were loyal to Vort out of fear more than honor, but to hear it so plainly laid out made her heart swell. Maybe there was hope after all, perhaps she could turn them against their commanders.

Taj put a hand on the alien's shoulder and gave a firm but gentle squeeze. "I promise you that no more harm will come to you as long as you cooperate." Cabe stood nearby, and though the alien couldn't see him, the Furlorian held a bolt pistol aimed at the soldier's chest.

The alien let out a resigned sigh and licked at his broad green lips. "Then ask your questions, alien, and I'll do my best to provide you with answers, though you need to understand that Captain Vort and Commander Dard are the two who truly know the most. They kept us grunts in the dark." His tail swished against the floor, hard scales scraping against stone.

Taj had figured as much, but it was worth a shot anyway. "What's your name? S'lorth?" she asked, vaguely remembering one of the other aliens calling it out.

"S'thlor," the soldier answered. "Private S'thlor."

"How many of you are there here?" Grady asked, sidling in closer. Taj resisted the urge to hiss at the old Tom for intruding, but she bit it back. She'd never interrogated anyone before, so maybe Grady knew more than she did.

"Maybe three hundred strong at this point, though probably a few less," S'thlor answered without any hesitance. "We lost a number of our crew in the attack that left us crippled and landed us here, not to mention the attack on the shuttles."

The alien soldier chuckled, a crooked smile stretching his lips. "That Federation bitch did us real harm, batting the *Monger* aside like an errant child. She left us bleeding atmosphere and lives until we were able to seal the back quarters and restore life support."

"Federation bitch?" Taj asked.

The alien chuckled. "You haven't heard of Queen Bethany Anne of the Federation?"

The resultant murmur and shuffle of feet made it clear they hadn't.

"Well, be grateful you haven't," S'thlor said. "She makes Grand Admiral Galforin look like a wet nurse. She's taken out more of our people in the last few cycles than any of our historical enemies combined." S'thlor drew in a slow, deep breath. "Her and her people have expanded into space from some unknown dirtball planet said to be named Earth. They've brought their gift for war to the stars and pity those who stand in her way."

Taj sat back on her heels a moment, letting her thoughts wander. This queen sounded fierce and cruel and uncompromising, but Taj had to remember who provided the information.

How much of what the alien said was truth, and how much of it was propaganda spewed by his command? Taj couldn't know unless she pressed the alien for more information regarding the Federation and its leaders, but now was not the time.

"Okay, so if we take Captain Vort and his commander out of the fight..." she hesitated to think about killing them, "would the rest of your brethren stand down?"

"Hardly," S'thlor answered. "As little love as they have for the captain, there is much terror for the actions of the grand admiral. You'll have men celebrating Vort's death, but it won't slow down the work that needs to be done."

"Why is that?" Lina asked, joining the questioning.

"Vort radioed home soon after we cashed here. Grand Admiral Galforin already knows the value of your planet and will let nothing stand in his way in his efforts to claim it as his own."

"Value?" Cabe scratched at a folded ear. "What value does this dirty scrub planet have to you?"

S'thlor shook his head. "You people are clueless," he said, letting out a quiet chuckle. "Your soil is infested with a mineral we call Toradium-42. That sparkly, silvery material you find right below the surface."

"And?"

"And," S'thlor replied, "it's pure energy. It's encapsulated in the tiniest, most compact source in the known universes, ready to be put to use with the barest of chemical adjustments. It can be prepared in days, and a handful of the stuff could power a Wyyvan superdreadnought for a cycle." He patted the ground beside him, kicking up dust. "Imagine what a planet steeped in the stuff could do?"

Taj could, and it made her stomach roil. That was what they had been searching for, why they'd been drilling into the planet, and why they'd been so adamant about taking out the locals. The Furlorians were nothing more than an inconvenience in their quest for the mineral they could use to power their warships.

"Better still, it's a completely stable energy source, and there has never been such an ample supply of Toradium-42 available anywhere else in the universe, to my knowledge." The alien shook his head. "So, no, even if you kill Vort and Dard, there's no escaping the Wyyvan machine bent upon stripping this planet bare."

"So, your people are coming for us no matter what?" Cabe asked.

Taj heard Em and Grady sigh behind her at the alien's nod. Lina hunkered down beside her.

"If you've got a way off the planet, I'd suggest you use it before Captain Vort finds it. Otherwise, it's a matter of time until each and every one of you is hunted down and killed. He doesn't care about you or your people, and he'll do anything to get into the Grand Admiral's good graces. As long as there are some of you left to make him look bad in front of the admiral, he will do everything in his power to torment and murder you."

Taj swallowed back the bile that had risen in her throat. She'd expected the captive to be willing to speak, given the alien's relationship to its captain, but she hadn't expected such brutal honesty from him. It shook her, setting a chill deep within her spine, which radiated out, tingling through her extremities.

After several long moments of silence, she waved Cabe to seize the alien. "Take him somewhere and lock him up for now. Be sure he's fed and treated well, but I don't want anyone else in there with him without my permission, understood?"

She cast a furtive glance at Gran Em and Grady. While she certainly didn't expect them to defy her and do anything that would put the Furlorians at risk, she knew they didn't approve of her holding S'thlor hostage.

He had no trade value, and what little information he knew he'd probably already spewed, so that left him as little more than one more mouth to feed in the face of an enemy who clearly had no intention of leaving anytime soon.

Cabe grunted his agreement and helped the alien to his feet. The pair shuffled off, into the gloom of the tunnels. Gran Em and Grady shuffled after him. Taj sighed as she watched them go, glancing over at Lina once they disappeared.

The little engineer got to her feet and dusted her uniform off. "What do we do now?"

Taj shrugged. "I don't know yet. We need to sit down and discuss some things. You and..." her voice trailed off as her brain shifted gears unconsciously.

Her head snapped about on her neck as though it were a swivel, peering into each and every crevice of their stone hideaway, not finding what she was looking for.

"What is it?" Lina asked, clearly catching the manic fervor of Taj's movements.

"Torbon," she whispered, straining to remember the last time she'd seen the Tom. "Where is Torbon?"

It was only then that Taj realized he hadn't been with them since they'd gone to sleep the night before.

"Bloody Rowl," She muttered, starting off down the tunnel. "Where the gack could he have gone?"

Before the sentence even cleared her lips, she already had a pretty good idea.

CHAPTER TWENTY-ONE

Taj burst from the desert hatch and bolted toward town, barely allowing Cabe and Lina to keep up. Though the sun hung high in the afternoon sky, the crew ran as if it were pure darkness. Torbon hadn't given them many options.

Taj swallowed the dust building in her throat and gnawed at the gritty sand between her teeth, but she never stopped running. Crouched low, she darted between buildings and clung to the shadows as best she could, staying as silent as she could. She had no clue what Torbon planned, but she was sure it'd be something none of them were prepared for. And that wasn't good.

Torbon had always been the odd one out, choosing a path most Furlorians wouldn't even think of taking even in the most mundane of situations. And while that might well be an asset in their fight against the invaders, his ideas were every bit as much a surprise to the enemy as they were to the crew.

There was no telling what he would do in his quest to rescue Jadie, but Taj was certain it would be something over the top, something that would put the crew on their heels as much as it did the aliens.

And that was dangerous.

With no idea what Torbon planned, Taj and the others could do nothing more than react and hope they ended up doing the right thing. *We probably won't,* she thought as she raced toward the most obvious of Torbon's targets, hoping to head him off before he did anything too stupid.

She felt sure they wouldn't make it.

He'd had all night to plot and plan and let his mind stew and run wild. Taj knew Jadie and her rescue was his goal, but beyond that, she knew nothing else, and it bothered her. At any moment—

And right then, as if Torbon had read her thoughts, she stumbled to a halt, Lina and Cabe skittering to a stop behind her. "You feel that?" she asked.

Cabe shook his head, but Lina groaned and nodded. "The ground's shaking."

Cabe caught onto the feeling a moment later. "Feels like they're drilling hard."

"That's not what that is." Taj inched toward the nearest corner and glanced around, her gaze filling with the swirl of a dirt-brown cloud that threatened to engulf the eastern side of Culvert City. Cabe and Lina crept alongside her, staring over her shoulder.

"What the gack is that?" Cabe asked as the ground continued to rumble.

"If I had to guess, I'd say this is Torbon's plan, whatever it is."

Both Cabe and Lina grunted, frozen in place by the massive cloud that devoured the city, block by block.

"We need to get to the barns," Taj told them, shaking them free of their lethargy as she bolted off again.

This time, there was no effort spent lurking or creeping. Instead, she ran full-out, not caring if the aliens saw her. If they had a gram of sense, they'd be indoors, dodging what it was setting the earth to trembling and the sky to swirling.

Taj was beginning to understand the scope of what Torbon had done, having experienced something similar when she was a kitten. *Bloody Rowl, Torbon.*

Paws scraping in the dirt, she skidded to a juddering stop alongside the last of the buildings nearest to the barns, the same one she'd used for reconnaissance when she'd first learned of the shuttle hiding within its walls.

She hoped the three of them wouldn't trip the shuttle's scanners as they clambered up the roof to settle in somewhere they could watch and be off the ground at the same time. As long as the interference was great enough, they could go unnoticed.

"Oh, Torbon," Lina muttered. "What have you done?" She stared out at the pens in the distance, hand over her eyes, as the sandy storm raced ever closer. Shapes appeared in the gloom not long after, and the panicked mewling of the balborans rose to drone out nearly every other sound.

Taj gulped. "He's started a stampede," she mumbled, realizing how far he'd gone in order to rescue his aunt.

"How did he do that?" Cabe asked, but the answer to his question became obvious a moment later as the first of the herd careened down Main Street.

Taj shuddered and pulled back from the ledge of the shaking building, as her vision sorted the images she spotted in the street below. "Gacking ferion spiders."

There, amidst the stampeding herd, were the telltale signs of the chest-sized, metallic spiders that infested some of the higher trees on Krawlas. The creatures skittered and climbed over the backs of the balborans, biting and stirring fear, glistening webs trailing like streamers from the horns of the oldest balborans.

"I can't watch," Lina said, and Taj agreed, though she found herself peeking over the ledge once more, watching as the herd of balborans hurtled past.

Alien soldiers, still clearly unsure as to what they were facing, spilled into the streets to confront the new threat. They regretted it instantly.

The muscled, meaty balborans, spurred on by terror, didn't so much as recognize the soldiers before they plowed into them. Aliens screamed and cried as they were run down, the great beasts shattering armor and bones without deference. Both snapped as the aliens were run down.

Those with their wits about them freed their weapons and fired into the wave of creatures, and while a number of the normally passive animals stumbled and fell beneath the onslaught, there was simply too much momentum to defy. Soldiers disappeared in the brownish clouds, trampled and crushed beneath the stampeding herd.

Taj fought back the urge to cheer as she saw how much damage the herd was doing. The stampede had already taken its toll on a number of older buildings, destroying the chance for the city itself to escape more harm. A few of the buildings had been rocked apart to tumble piece by piece in the street. It was hardly consequential given what the invaders had already done with their initial assault.

Thought it hurt her to see how much damage was being done, she consoled herself with the thought that the buildings could be repaired, rebuilt, and were hardly a big deal in the grand scheme of things. As long as her people survived, they would be fine, even if it meant they would have to start all over.

It wouldn't be the first time, she thought. They could do it.

She grinned at Torbon's wayward ingenuity as she watched the storm of balborans plow through Main Street, tearing through the enemy soldiers without hesitance or concern for retaliation.

Then she cast her glance toward the barn that held her people, knowing that, any moment from now, Torbon would appear and make his move to free the hostages. She and the crew needed to be ready to help when he did.

That's when she heard the burst of shuttle engines rattling to their west. She glanced over a shoulder only to see the craft appear almost out of nowhere, dark gray against the glistening blue of the sky, and adjust its course.

It darted over Main Street and spun about one hundred eighty degrees. Taj could hear the whines of its guns spooling up and watched as it let loose on the herd, blasting balborans and ferion spiders indiscriminately.

It was likely the craft was even killing some of its own people in the attack, desperate to bring a halt to the stampede at any cost as it chewed up the road with its guns.

Great bolts of gleaming green energy tore into the animals, and blood and charred viscera exploded, spewing into the sky. Thumps and thuds echoed throughout town as bits of meat and gristle spattered the nearby buildings, coating them in bloody paint and gore.

Within moments, the herd had come to an abrupt halt near the front. The back end pushed in hard, slowing the forward motion and giving the shuttle more and more targets to pile lifeless in town.

The soldiers had finally retreated and scattered back into the cover of the nearby buildings. They provided cover fire from their shelters, helping to halt the stampede and limit further impact.

Taj snarled, knowing their time was coming to a close. She stared at the barn where her people were being held, yet she saw no activity there, nothing that would indicate Torbon had been angling to free their people, and she wondered why not?

Why wasn't he there? What had happened to him?

A million things churned inside her skull in an instant, none of them good. Her stomach roiled as she stared on. Soldiers still stood their posts about the barn, weapons up and firing into the herd, but there was no other movement to show that Torbon was attempting to break in.

Taj gritted her teeth and did her best to think like Torbon, to determine what he might have in mind, but there was no way she could manage it, her own thoughts too orderly, too composed to mimic the chaos inside Torbon's brain.

And then she caught the first clue as to his real plan. "Oh, gack."

There was a muffled *thump* of engines firing nearby, and Taj scanned the area, catching a glimpse of red-orange as it flashed inside the nearest of the barns, flames sputtering between the slats, charring the wood.

She tapped Lina on the shoulder and asked, "Did you see that?"

The engineer nodded, but by then, everyone had seen it, the back of the barn having caught on fire.

A loud roar erupted, and the doors on the nearest barn burst open, exploding from their hinges to be hurled aside, adding to the maelstrom in the street outside.

The shuttle the enemy had hidden inside the barn broke free of its confines and veered hard upward, rising at almost a perfectly vertical climb. Taj screamed despite herself as she calculated the trajectory and realized where it was angled.

Right toward the other shuttle.

"There's no way—" she muttered, but there very clearly was.

The damaged shuttle shot upwards like a missile, trailing orange. The other shuttle barely had time to recognize the danger it was in. It wasn't enough time to react. The shuttles collided with a *boom* that echoed like thunder over Culvert City.

Lina shrieked, and Cabe pulled her in tight, forcing her head away from the collision so she couldn't see it. Taj, however, stared on, transfixed.

The front of Torbon's shuttle crashed into the engines of the other, crippling both ships as steel warped and crumpled as if it were paper. The two shuttles veered off out of control, the enemy's spinning away to slam into the ground near the balborans pens. It hit with a brutal *thud*, and the ship imploded, devouring itself from within, great red flares shooting from it and marking its final destination.

The shuttle Torbon piloted fared little better.

It spun away toward the desert, tumbling end over end, little more than a blur against the blue backdrop of the sky. Out amongst the scrub and hard soil, it met the end of its arc and toppled to earth, striking with a sullen *thump*. An explosion followed.

Taj gave in, at last, and howled, dropping to her knees as a column of black smoke rose up from the crash site.

"Torbon!"

CHAPTER TWENTY-TWO

"I have to admit, I did not expect *that*," Captain Vort said, staring at the view screen in the small transport he used to return to the ship. Soldiers raced alongside, weapons at the ready.

Commander Dard nodded. "Nor I," he admitted.

Vort let out a quiet breath and continued to stare at his screen, twin columns of smoke marking where the shuttles had gone down. He'd underestimated the commitment of the Furlorians to their people. Turning loose a stampede of feed creatures to lay ruin to the town and kill his soldiers was a surprise. Worse still, it was an effective one.

"How many men did we lose?"

The commander paused a moment, Vort imagining he was running the numbers on his visor screen, then he grunted. "Fifty-six dead, one-hundred-twelve wounded in some small manner or another," Dard said. "Most of the deaths and injuries occurred at the onset, when the herd drove through the drill field before the men had identified what was going on, then in town where our forces attempted to identify and nullify the threat. I've ordered a field triage to be erected near the primary drill site to tend to them and minimize the drain on the *Monger*'s resources."

"And the equipment?" Vort asked, wondering how much time the Furlorians' little stunt had cost him. The loss of the shuttles was bad enough, reducing how much Toradium-42 they could transport back to the *Monger*, but if the drill equipment itself was compromised, it would ruin all his plans entirely.

"Fortunately, most of the drills and bits were salvaged, having been withdrawn for maintenance and cooling operations," Dard answered, and Vort let his head loll inside his helmet, grateful for a piece of good news, at last. "We lost a few rigs, the machinery flattened in the rush, but our total impact is hardly affected. I'm more worried about delivery. Without our shuttles, we've little means of carting the mineral to the *Monger*."

Captain Vort nodded. He pictured making the little aliens suffer, making them ferry the Toradium-42 to the ship by hand, but that presented a logistical nightmare. It would take far too many of his resources to cover the Furlorians to ensure they didn't escape or do something untoward regarding the mineral. It also left the captives exposed, giving the remaining rebel element opportunities to free them. Vort certainly didn't want that.

"Bring the *Monger* closer," he decided.

"In its condition, sir?"

Vort chuckled. "The ship is hardly air-worthy, I'll admit, but a short distance move shouldn't impact the integrity of the craft too much. Build thrust slow and stay close to the ground, and I don't imagine there will be any issues we can't overcome." He glanced out the wind screen, off into the desert where the *Monger* sat. "As long as life support and general functions remain intact, then our quality of life here will not be affected. That's all that matters."

Dard nodded. Vort knew the commander understood their position. With the Monger unable to return to space, they were dependent upon Grand Admiral Galforin's assistance. Until they were provided with a backup crew and better drilling equipment, Vort's goal was to subjugate and control the local population and obtain as much Toradium-42 as possible, given the circumstances.

He didn't need the Monger for much more than shelter and storage. *Realistically,* he thought, keeping his amusement to himself, *as long as my quarters remain intact, I'm happy.*

The rest of the forces can sleep in town, if need be, until Galforin sends reinforcements. By then, Vort would have a substantial private cache of Toradium-42 and could live out his days in comfort no matter the outcome.

He grinned and waved Commander Dard on. "Get me back to the Monger so we can get the ship moved closer," he told him. "And tell Kabal to be prepared for more fodder. Too many of the creatures still elude us, obviously. I want them carved to the bone until they give up the others, no mercy." Vort paused, letting his thoughts wash over him. "And gather a number of the hostages together. I think it's time for another demonstration."

Commander Dard offered a sharp nod, clearly passing along the order already through the private comm network.

Vort grinned. Though the locals had caught him off guard with their ingenuity, he blamed himself for their success. Up to now, he'd thought of them as little more than vermin to be exterminated at his leisure. Now that they'd shown him their true colors, he knew better.

He wouldn't underestimate them again. No, he'd spread their blood across the dirt from city border to border if he had to, but he couldn't afford to let the little rats make a fool of him again.

CHAPTER TWENTY-THREE

"Stop it, Taj," Cabe argued, his voice raw, and his words harsh. "If Torbon was in that shuttle, he's dead, plain and simple."

No matter how right she thought he was, she didn't want to believe it. "He can't be. H-he—"

A cold chill seemed to freeze her in place, goosebumps prickling the fur along her arms, and *thumped* her fists against his arms without energy. She didn't have it in her. Too many losses in too short a time, and Taj was feeling the effects of all of them.

Tears stung her eyes and matted the fur on her cheek, and no amount of wiping would clear them. But she wasn't alone in her grief. Though Cabe held her in place, doing his best to appear strong, his eyes glistened in the sunlight. He sniffed several times, trying to rein his emotions in, but there was little he could do.

Of all of them, Lina was the most composed, and Taj thought that was more due to shock than actual restraint.

She stared into the distance, the column of smoke from Torbon's crashed shuttle reflected in her wide eyes.

She stood without movement, only the barest flutter of her chest giving away that she still breathed. Taj was tempted to go over and shake the engineer to see if she was okay, but she couldn't bring herself to break free of Cabe. Though he barely held her, it was as if his hand were steel clamps.

Rather than continue to struggle, she pushed in closer and wrapped her arms around him, sinking her head into his warm chest. "H-he can't be…dead. He can't."

"You have to hope," Cabe told her, but she could tell he didn't believe what he was saying and was only trying to pacify her.

It didn't make her feel any better, but she appreciated the effort, nonetheless. Still, she couldn't get Torbon out of her head.

"What if he's hurt, trapped inside the shuttle?" She felt him go limp in her arms.

"What if he isn't?"

Taj groaned. She hated when he turned things around on her. She pulled away, huffed, and raised a claw his direction, but he cut her off before she got a chance to say anything.

"I'll go check," he said, "but there's no way we can all go." Cabe waved a hand in the general direction of the routed stampede, soldiers milling about and redirecting the balborans back the way they came. "Won't be long before they have things back under control, and we can't all be sneaking around seeing how they're gonna be on high alert, especially now. We'll be caught."

Taj sighed. She'd had grand plans of using Torbon's distraction to free the captives, but despite it all, nothing had really changed all that much. There were still too many soldiers guarding her people, too little opportunity to get something done that made sense. Right now, they were sitting out in the open, arguing about what to do. If it weren't for the chaos still being tamped down, the aliens would have spotted them already.

They would soon enough, Taj knew. She let out a loud sigh and agreed with Cabe, much as she wanted to kick, scream, and argue. There wasn't any point in it all.

"Yeah, please, check on him, just in case." She hated thinking Torbon was dead, but she had seen how the shuttle had been piloted. He *must* have been inside, and if he was, it was highly unlikely he'd made it through the crash. She couldn't bring herself to admit it out loud. It simply hurt too much after all they'd been through.

Cabe nodded. "Go back to the tunnels," he told her. "I'll be back in a while to let you know what I find." He darted off without another word, disappearing into the dusty city, weaving his way between alleys.

After he'd gone, Taj stood there, staring in the direction he'd gone, doing her best to ignore the black column of smoke that was his destination. After a few long moments, Lina came over beside her. Taj turned to the engineer.

"You see that?"

Taj shook her head and stared off in the direction Lina pointed. At first, she could see nothing but the haze of dust kicked up by the balborans, but then a loud rumble helped draw her focus. The clouds swelled, and then were blown aside, a great orange fire clearing them away in a rush.

"Oh...gack!"

Taj's heart rose to form a knot in her throat as she watched the alien destroyer fire its engines and rise slowly into the air. The sleek beast of a spacecraft crept upward in defiance of gravity. Taj thrilled at seeing it, realizing her hopelessness against the monstrosity built for war.

"Are they going to—?" She couldn't bring herself to ask the question as the Monger shifted slowly and turned toward Culvert City.

"I don't know," Lina answered, seeming to understand what Taj had meant to ask.

Would they turn their guns on Culvert City? had been the question Taj was too afraid to ask.

She could see it happening, especially after her brilliant plan to attack the shuttles, followed by Torbon loosing a stampede and wrecking the last of the shuttles. Nothing to lose by raining down fire on the city. Taj imagined Captain Vort scorching Culvert City into ash with his destroyer's weapons.

"Can they hit the tunnels?" Taj asked.

Lina nodded in her peripheral vision. "At this range, they'd blast holes a hundred meters deep or more. There'd be nothing left of Culvert City and the tunnels but a smoldering crater."

"You're not making me feel any better about this," Taj muttered. The massive ship grew larger and larger as it moved in their direction, blocking out the sun. "We've got to warn everyone."

Lina clamped a hand on her arm. "It's too late," she whispered, her voice barely carrying past the roar of the destroyer's fluttering engines. "We'd never make it to the tunnels in time, let alone inside." Lina pulled Taj aside, drawing them deeper into the shadows of the alley they hid within. "This is the end, Taj."

Taj pulled her friend into her side, clasping her tight as the warship drew closer and closer. She hadn't realized how quickly the thing moved until she noticed it was nearly above them. It had been only moments, and she knew Lina was right.

Even if they had made it to the catacombs, there was no way they'd have ushered all its inhabitants to the western hatch and out of the tunnels before the ship let loose its destructive energies.

Taj sobbed and pulled her friend even closer. "I love you, Lina."

"I love you, too," the engineer answered and, finally, she, too, let out a quiet sob, muffling the sound with the back of her hand. "It's probably better for them this way," she managed to say, nearly choking on the words. "Fast, painless..."

Right then, a great bark erupted from one of the ship's engines, and Taj watched as it flickered and failed, staining the sky with blackened fumes. The ship groaned, steel creaking, and dropped in a graceful fall toward the earth. Taj clasped Lina even tighter, and the pair watched as the destroyer changed its angle and *thumped* heavily in the open plain outside of town.

The ground jumped beneath their feet and nearly knocked them apart, but they clung to each other until the earth stopped rattling. Wreckage already damaged by the invasion and the stampede clattered from buildings and toppled to the ground. Bits of debris showered down like wooden rain, but with the streets empty, it did little harm.

Taj sucked a deep breath into her stinging lungs and let it out loudly. Her knees trembled, and only her tight hold of Lina kept her from falling over. "Bloody Rowl," she muttered, staring at the giant destroyer now parked on the other side of town, her legs wobbling under her. "I thought we were done for."

Lina nodded her agreement, her ear tickling Taj's nose as she slipped free of her friend's grasp. She inched forward, peering around the corner of the alleyway, clearly assessing the alien ship.

"Why do you think they didn't raze the town?" Taj asked.

"I don't think they can." Lina spun, a grin splitting her lips, teeth sparkling. "I bet their guns are out." She gestured toward the *Monger*. "While I can understand them holding back initially, not being certain as to what they were getting into, why would they hold back now?"

"They wouldn't."

"Exactly," Lina confirmed. "We've been nothing but trouble to them since they arrived, and they've shown they're more than willing to kill our people without hesitation. So, that makes me think the guns on their ship don't work, or they would have used them on us already." Lina sighed. "Well, at least they're likely not working for now. They could be busy repairing them."

"Yeah, just what I wanted to hear," Taj muttered, staring at the destroyer as it settled into the dirt. "Maybe they don't want to destroy any of that weird mineral they've been mining," she countered. "Could it be worth that much to them? More than our lives?"

Lina shrugged. "They're throwing more of their people and resources into it rather than trying to capture us, so yeah, seems to make sense that it is. Gack, for all I know, it could be explosive, and they don't want to blow the entire region up, especially since they are stranded here."

"Also, not something I wanted to hear," Taj told her friend. The idea that they were sitting on a field of minerals that could explode made her blood run cold. "Maybe we should—"

A loud, metallic *clank* drew their attention back to the ship. Like when they'd first encountered it, they watched as the loading hatch hummed and eased open. Taj clambered up the side of the building to get a better view.

She hadn't so much as settled in when she spied the alien captain exit the ship. Alongside him walked his commander and a small army of soldiers, the group forming a tight circle around a cluster of captive Furlorians.

As before, they strode with their heads down, shoulders slumped. The whole group made a slow, steady march toward the town square, as they had the last time the captain had done this.

Taj hissed and dropped back to the ground beside Lina, landing heavily.

"What is it?" the engineer asked.

"He's getting ready to kill more of our people," she answered, her fists so tight her claws dug into her palms. "I can't watch this, not again."

Lina glanced around the corner, off toward the

destroyer. After a quiet moment, she sighed and turned back to face Taj. "I've an idea."

"Am I gonna like it?"

Lina shook her head. "Probably not."

Taj grunted, hearing the group of aliens and their captives moving ever closer to the town square, to their inevitable death. "Gack it. I'm in."

CHAPTER TWENTY-FOUR

"I knew I wasn't gonna like this," Taj whispered, letting out a slow, quiet breath.

She and Lina inched around the massive steel plates of armor that blocked them from view of the two guards patrolling the *Monger*'s gangplank. The aliens stood there at lazy inattention, neither looking as if he took his duty all that seriously. Taj could understand why.

Who in their right mind would dare try to break into the destroyer, not knowing how many soldiers or crew remained aboard?

She caught herself raising her hand and dragged it back to her side. Taj was clearly not in her right mind, and of all the crazy things she'd done since the invaders set foot on Krawlas, this was, by far, the most insane, and she had Lina to thank for it.

Taj wasn't even sure what they hoped to accomplish by it, anyway. It wasn't as if the two of them could take over and secure the ship, even if they found it empty, which Taj was sure it wasn't.

Captain Vort and his commander might have left, and S'thlor might have told them the *Monger* was being manned by a skeleton crew most times since the mineral had been uncovered, but how long would the captain be gone? How much of what the captive alien had told them was truth?

She didn't have the answer to either question. That made her nervous.

"Seriously, Lina, what are we doing here?"

"We need to know what we're up against, don't we? Why the ship didn't blow us all to Rowl, what kind of time we have before the alien cavalry shows up, and the answers to a million questions we haven't even begun to think of yet." Lina tapped a quiet palm against the ship's hull. "All that's in here, in the databanks and system memory."

"And if we get caught?"

"Then we get caught." Lina shrugged. "Outside of us sneaking off in the dark and leaving everyone behind, do you see anything resembling a happy ending here?"

Taj grunted. "And here I thought Torbon was the pessimist."

"We've gotta do something, Taj. No matter what happens, we're running out of time."

Offering a shallow nod, Taj agreed without saying a word. Though she would have preferred to do this a different way and spend a little more time doing recon to know what they were walking in on, Lina's statement echoed Taj's thoughts. There was no time to waste. It was now or never.

Taj waited until the soldiers turned their back to the

two Furlorians, the men chatting casually and doing their best to pass the time, and she darted out from the concealing hull and bolted for the lowered gangplank. Lina was hot on her heels.

As soon as Taj slipped beneath the steel walkway, she cast a furtive glance in the soldiers' direction. Once she was sure they were still occupied, caught up in the mundane boredom of service, she clambered up the bottom of the gangplank. She used her claws to hold her fast to the aerated steel, allowing her to climb the walkway on the backside of it, out of view. Lina followed close behind.

These aliens have never encountered a race like us, Taj thought with a chuckle. Not to mention they'd likely never had to wage a guerilla-style fight before either.

With the Furlorians stealth and grace, the pair were able to scamper along the supports of the gangplank, only climbing onto the upper side at the top, where they slipped inside the ship without notice.

It didn't hurt that the destroyer's scanners were even more finite than those of the shuttles. While they could most certainly pick out life forms from orbit, there was no way for them to identify singular targets parked as they were on a planet. They were effectively blind, only aiding the pair's sneaky entry into the craft.

Once inside, Taj took a split-second to catch her breath, the air hitching anxiously in her lungs, but Lina was a burst of activity.

"Come on," the engineer whispered. "We can't sit around here. There's no telling how many patrols they have on duty inside. We need to get in and out fast."

Taj couldn't agree more. "Lead the way."

Lina did, despite the fact that she'd never before been on a ship like this. Still, Taj trusted the tiny engineer's instincts. With her hand on the wall, Lina jotted down corridor after corridor, as if she were being led by the ship itself. Taj grinned. That might well be true. But even if it weren't, she still had to know better than Taj. To her, every gray hallway looked the same.

She sniffed along the path, drawing in the various smells and aromas of the alien ship, dragging a paw here and there to mark it, doing her best to keep the scents straight so she could find her way out if need be, but there was simply no way it would happen if she had to rely on sight alone. The ship was simply too uniform, too rigid in appearance to allow her to grasp her location well.

It was as she scrambled to unravel the labyrinth of the *Monger* that the shuffle of booted feet caught her off guard. Her heart sparked into a gallop, and she spun about as shadows darkened the converging corridor, voices muttering.

Then there was a hiss, and a hand clasped her biceps and yanked her backward through a door she hadn't even realized had been there. A second hiss sounded right after, and Taj gasped as she was pressed against the cold steel wall, Lina's paw over her mouth. Narrow eyes demanded silence. The two stood there, locked together, until Lina eased back, at last, letting Taj go.

"You need to keep it together, Taj," Lina whispered. "There might not be much in the way of patrols, but if you walk right into one…" She let her warning hang, and Taj nodded.

"Sorry. Got a little distracted by all this." She waved her arms about to encompass the whole of the ship.

"I understand," Lina replied, this time not putting as much effort into keeping her voice muted. "Good thing we're here already."

Taj straightened and glanced about, the tiny room they were in as uniform and samey as the previous corridors, only smaller. "What is this place?"

Lina grinned. "For lack of a better name, the command core."

"This?" Taj glanced around again, shaking her head, unimpressed. "Not gonna lie, but this looks more like a janitorial closet than any technological ship hub."

"Which is why I'm the engineer and you're the officer-in-training." Lina grinned wide, teeth gleaming.

"Probably true," Taj admitted. "So, what is it you want here?"

Lina shrugged. "Not sure yet. I'm hoping to plug into the database and see what intel I can download, give us a better idea as to what this ship's current capabilities are and anything else we can about the aliens."

"So, you're pretty much digging through their belongings in hope of stumbling across something?"

"Pretty much, yeah."

Taj chuckled. The fact that they had sneaked aboard the alien spaceship was crazy enough, but now that they were rummaging about in search of Rowl knows what, Taj couldn't wrap her head around the lunacy of what they were doing.

"I don't know about this," she said, watching as Lina

wasted no time and began fiddling with various panels. "How long is this gonna take you?"

"Minutes…hours." Lina raised a furred eyebrow. "I really don't know. All of this is, forgive the pun, *alien* to me."

Taj groaned. "Had to go there, huh?"

Lina grinned and kept working, peeling back panel after panel and examining the electronics behind them. Not more than a moment later, she was absorbed in her task.

After watching without any comprehension of what the engineer was attempting to accomplish, Taj grew antsy, her brain wandering off of its own accord. She realized they'd made this opportunity for themselves and would likely never be able to take advantage of it again.

"I'll meet you back here in a bit," she muttered and slipped out the door and back into the hallway before Lina could argue.

Already aboard, risking being caught and killed every second they were there, it only made sense to make the most of it. The door hissed behind her, and Taj darted off down the hallway in the direction they were headed before they stumbled across the patrol.

As before, she marked her passage and trailed that of the alien soldiers, their musky scents a strong tether toward keeping her focused and headed in what she presumed would be a good direction to be moving.

The task of the soldiers was to guard the ship, and it only made sense they would patrol the most important areas. They'd already traipsed past the engineering section, where Lina played happily, so Taj figured the next area in line would be the bridge or the armory or something similarly important. It wasn't logical that the aliens would guard the kitchens or sleeping areas, so she chased the scent of the aliens, trailing them in their arc around the ship.

It was only when the coppery stink of blood intruded that she stumbled to a halt.

A door with a small porthole in its face stood open a crack, and Taj realized that was where the smell emanated. Another door hung open a short distance farther, both set in a dead-end corridor. A quiet murmur sounded from the far room, and Taj pressed herself against the wall, drawing quick breaths through lips that were peeled back.

She could hear the shuffle of feet and a muttered voice echoing down the hallway, and though it was quiet and seemed content to remain in place, if anyone stepped out right then, there was nowhere she could run or hide. She'd be spotted in an instant.

Her mind begged for her to flee, and her feet nearly complied, but the thick scent of Furlorian held her in place. Whatever was going on there involved her people, and no amount of fear could spur her into flight until she found out what was going on.

Though the logical side of her brain did its best to convince her that she knew exactly what was happening there and what she would find, it did nothing to stop her feet from pressing forward.

She clasped her bolt pistol and moved to the cracked door. She drew in a deep breath and peeled the door open wide enough for her, and she slipped inside the dark chamber.

She regretted her decision instantly.

The stink of death and decay struck as she entered the room, which she immediately recognized as a prison of sorts. She choked back a retch, and pushed on, staying close to the wall to keep her away from the row of small cages and allow her as much room to maneuver as possible, given the narrow confines. Were anyone to walk inside, it would take them a moment to see her, and she might be able to slip free before they even noticed she was there.

At least that was what she'd thought until she spied who occupied the cells.

Her stomach churned as she caught sight of several Furlorians, people she knew from town, hunched over and locked inside the cells. They looked battered and bruised and, in the case of several, ready to curl up and let Rowl take them. None that she could tell were awake or conscious, each lying in a pool of their own blood and filth.

"What are you doing here?" a raspy voice asked from the center-most cage.

Taj stiffened and caught a blur of movement as one of the Furlorians opened her eyes and stared out at Taj. It took a few seconds, the swollen wreckage of the woman's face distorting her features, but Taj realized who it was: Gran Lee, an elder who'd been friends with Mama Merr since the flight from Felinus 4.

Taj raced to the cage, clasping the bars as though she might rip them loose from their moorings. "I need to get you out of here."

The old Gran shook her head, though the movement was barely noticeable given her obvious weakness. "No, child, there'll be none of that," she said, her raspy voice a barren desert long devoid of moisture. "We're already dead."

Taj choked on a sob, her eyes wandering the cages of their own accord, confirming the Gran's statement. None of the other Furlorians did much more than shudder or twitch. This close to them, Taj could smell the end upon them, each clinging to life more out of habit than desire. They had been broken, each and every one of them.

The thought set fire to Taj's tears, sending them steaming away from her eyes. She wanted to rip Captain Vort's throat out, make him pay for what he'd done to her people, make him suffer. Her mind filled with a million ideas of torment and torture, how she'd make Vort suffer, but all that was derailed as Gran Lee eased a hand through the bars and clasped Taj's leg.

"Now is not the time for revenge, child," she managed to say, startling Taj back to the present.

"Then when is?"

Lee forced the barest of smiles at that but shook her head. "Those of us here will not surrender anything to these invaders," she said, "but their torturer is crafty. It's only a matter of time before someone gives in to his wiles and reveals where our people hide away, child."

She gestured toward the room farther down the hall with a limp wave. "You must get our people and flee before they stumble upon that person and more of us suffer. Find Mama and Beaux, get them to safety, then worry about putting a hole in this captain's chest."

The mention of Mama and Gran Beaux snuffed the fury Taj felt, filling her eyes with tears once more. Still, she held her tongue and said nothing to the old Gran. If she didn't know Beaux and Mama were dead, Taj sure as gack wouldn't let that be her last memory. She simply nodded.

"I can't leave you here, though," Taj muttered, letting her hands examine the bars in search of a way to open them. But before she managed that, she heard voices in the hall outside.

"Go, child," Gran Lee told her. "I'm done, but you have a mission before you, which must be fulfilled. Do not let foolishness land you here with me." She drew a deep, trembling breath and waved. "Go."

As if on instinct, Taj turned her back on the old Gran, though it sent waves of fire arcing through her heart, and she ran to the cracked door. She peered outside as two alien soldiers stalked past. Taj stiffened, pinning herself against the wall, her bolt pistol clasped so tight in her hands that her knuckles ached. She held her breath, crouched low, ready to pounce.

Fortunately, she didn't have to.

The complaining soldiers kept on, marching down the hall, and then turning into the room at the end of the corridor before vanishing from sight. Taj let the stale air gush from her lungs and turned to face the old Gran one last time.

"I'll be back for you," she told her, though they both knew that was likely a white lie, spoken more for comfort than anything else. Gran Lee offered a somber nod, relieving Taj of her obligation without a word, and let her head drop the floor once more.

Taj swallowed a sob and bolted from the room before the soldiers emerged from the other to spot her. She wiped her nose on the back of her paw, clearing it to better scent her way back the way she'd come.

Ears flickering, on alert, she raced back toward where she'd left Lina. She came across the engineer as Lina left the command core room, the two hissing as they nearly collided. Taj took a second to catch her breath, then asked, "Get what you needed?"

Lina grinned and nodded, patting a small, metallic cube tucked under her arm. "You?"

"Way more," Taj answered, unwilling to elaborate even when Lina pressed her. "Let's get out of here. We can catch up afterward."

Lina didn't argue, and the pair darted for the exit, slipping free of the *Monger* as easily as they'd boarded her because the two soldiers outside were still as distracted as ever.

It was a quiet journey back to the tunnels, and no matter how many times Lina nudged her for information, Taj couldn't bring herself to say anything. She couldn't get the image of Gran Lee and the others out of her mind, and she feared that, once she started talking, the tears would spill free and never stop.

So, instead, she held her tongue and made her way *home*, doing her best to ignore the alien Captain's voice that blared ominously through town over his loudspeaker. She twitched as blaster fire emphasized his every word, and she did her best to ignore the sound of her people dying and kept moving.

She could break down once she was there, she promised herself. If only for a little while.

CHAPTER TWENTY-FIVE

"If I have not made it clear, the games are over," Captain Vort shouted, letting his voice carry across the square.

He reached out and grabbed a Furlorian by its scruff, reveling in its hissing and moaning, and pressed the barrel of blaster pistol against the back of the creature's skull. He tapped the trigger without remorse, blowing a hole in the alien's head.

Blood splattered Vort's visor, dotting his vision, but that didn't deter the captain. In fact, it only motivated him. He let the dead alien drop and snatched another, doing the same and tossing the Furlorian's body into the dirt beside its brethren.

"I've no more patience for this," he said, turning about to ensure the entire city heard him, hidden or otherwise. "My torturer is working relentlessly at breaking the will of your people. It will not be long before these poor, broken souls surrender." He waved to Commander Dard, who stepped forward with a large, plastic bag.

Dard raised the bag and showed it about before untying the clasp. He held the bag over his head and dumped the contents out. Severed Furlorian fingers rained down, splattering as they hit the dirt. He moved back behind the captain once he was finished.

"This is your last warning," Vort called out, gesturing to the fingers. "Come sundown, I will offer no more mercy. Surrender or die."

Vort kicked the pile of fingers aside, scattering them over the street like gory party gifts, and then he spun about on his heel. His visor sealed, he stared grim at the alien town that surrounded him, hoping the locals would, at last, heed to his orders and give up.

Another unexpected move like the stampede and Vort would have too few men to take advantage of the lull before Grand Admiral Galforin's forces arrived and took control over Vort's Toradium-42 find.

After everything he'd been through, there was no way he would let that happen.

CHAPTER TWENTY-SIX

Taj did her best to ignore the nagging voice in her head that told her the alien captain had killed people while she ran, purposely avoiding town square as it happened. She'd enough guilt weighing her down already. Soon, she wouldn't have the strength to put one foot in front of the other for all the torment piled atop her shoulders.

To have witnessed who had been murdered, to see their faces and know who they were, would have broken her. Taj was against the wall, and she knew it. Wouldn't take much more to shatter her completely.

In the tunnels, at last, she found a quiet place to sit away from the hubbub of the rest of her people. She was unable to face them yet. Dropping to her butt with a sigh, her tail swished behind her as Lina plopped down beside her. She clutched the box she'd taken from the alien ship, her eyes never leaving it.

Rather than dwell on everything, her mind a tangle of

briars, she motioned her chin toward the box. "What is that thing?"

"This…this is a control cube," Lina answered. "I think."

"You think?"

"Well, the thing is alien, you know? I'm pretty sure, but it's gonna take some tinkering for me to get the hang of it."

"What does it do?" Taj asked. "You know that, at least?"

Lina chuckled. "Well, if I didn't mistakenly pick up a trash incinerator instead, this thing *should* allow me to remotely access some of the destroyer's basic functions once I make some adjustments."

"*Should?*"

"Alien tech, remember?" Lina fiddled with the box, turning it over in her hands. "If it works the way I think it does, it's basically a step down from an EI system. There's no sentience to it, fortunately, but it allows for a small crew to more effectively pilot and control the ship while freeing up people to do other things."

"Rampage and destroy, obviously."

"Sounds about right," Lina agreed. "But yeah, this thing is basically the operating system of the *Monger*, the computer that runs the computer."

"Can you fix the guns and use them through that?" Taj pointed at the box.

Lina shook her head. "Nope. Were the guns being used against us, I might be able to draw power from them, redirect it elsewhere, but fire control isn't integrated into the cube from what I can tell. That's a separate process, intentional redundancies in case something happens to this thing."

"Like nerdy little engineers getting their hands on it?"

"You know it." Lina chuckled, but her laughter was cut off by a shuffle of feet. Her eyes shot wide, and Taj spun about to see what had spooked her.

Cabe came around the corner, shadows flanking him. His grin was so bright it illuminated the tunnel with its gleam. "Look what I found." He stepped to the side and let the dark figures approach. Taj nearly choked as she scrambled to her feet.

There, whole and apparently healthy, stood Torbon, his grin twice as wide as Cabe's.

"What the gack!" Taj leapt at him, slamming him into the wall as she embraced him. "You're okay?"

Torbon chuckled. "I am," he answered, clearly enjoying the attention.

"But...we thought..."

Lina crashed into the pair, wrapping her arms around both Taj and Torbon, squeezing them for all she was worth.

"I was dead?" Torbon asked. "I thought maybe I was for a little while, too. I damn near didn't get out of the shuttle fast enough, but no, I made it." He reached up and touched a spot on his forehead where his fur had been scorched. "It was close, though, have to admit," he said with a grin.

"You scared the gack out of us," Taj screamed at him, pulling away and punching him in the arm. "Don't you ever do that again."

Torbon grunted and raised his hands in supplication. "Hey, that hurts. Is that how you treat a conquering hero?"

"Conquering hero, my tail," Lina muttered, following suit and punching him in the arm. "You scared us half to death."

"Well, I'm sorry," he replied, inching away from his furious crew members, "but I wouldn't take it back for anything." A grin slithered to his lips once more, and he stepped aside, allowing the crew to see the other shadow that come into the tunnel with him.

Taj stiffened, her breath catching in her throat. "J-Jadie?" Torbon's aunt smiled, wrinkles setting her whiskers to trembling. "You got her out?" Taj shouted, diving once more to hug Jadie, only pulling back at the last instant to keep from driving the woman into the wall.

"Bloody Rowl, it's great to see you. I was so worried they were gonna..." Taj let the sentence drift away, deciding it best not to spoil the moment with too much honesty. She squeezed Torbon's aunt tighter. "I'm so glad you're here."

"Me, too," she answered, grinning, seeming as unwilling to release Taj as Taj did her. They clung to each other, Lina joining the embrace a moment later. They simply stood there, hugging as if they might never let go.

It wasn't until Taj cleared her head and remembered how many other hostages there were in the barn that she eased away, guilt pecking at her like a murder of angry crows. "What about the others?" she asked Torbon.

His smile faltered at that. "I snuck out about ten others, but the soldiers must have realized it was all a distraction and circled back around to us. We barely made it into the desert before they sealed the barn off again. I-I..." he sucked in a deep breath, looking as if he wanted to break down and cry. "I couldn't get any more."

Taj leaned over and kissed him on the cheek. "You did great, apart from all the tail-poofing." She offered him a soft smile. "I'm glad to see you're okay." Taj looked over at Jadie. "Both of you. I truly am."

Jadie grabbed Torbon and pulled him close. "Me, too, nephew." Torbon grinned, nearly ear to ear.

"Yeah," Cabe said, his features somber, whiskers flat against his cheeks, "that's the best news we've had for a while. Likely to be the best we'll have for a while moving forward, too."

Lina sighed. "And the moment is ruined. Thanks, Cabe."

He shrugged. "Sorry, just being honest. We're not out of it yet."

Much as Taj wanted to argue, she couldn't. Cabe was right, and she hated it. His statement dragged her down into the mire once more, flooding her with all the emotions she'd fought so hard to shoulder aside.

"Anyone have any ideas?" Taj asked.

Jadie shuffled her feet. "Maybe I should go back and check on the others," she said, "leave you to your...meeting."

Taj smiled at her. Jadie had watched the crew grow up together and knew how close they were. It was almost impossible for her not to feel like an outsider among them, despite her closeness to the group. A number of years older, she'd always watched over them like children, but she'd left them to do what they did. That she felt the need to run off now didn't surprise Taj one bit.

"You're always welcome, of course," Taj replied, "but if you need to..."

Jadie nodded. "Yeah, I better. Need to update the Grans and let the others know what's going on up there." She smiled, shining its light over the crew in turn. "If you need anything, come get me."

Jadie gave them each a hug, letting Torbon linger in her arms for a bit before she finally let go and made her way down the tunnel. The crew watched her until she vanished.

After she was gone, Cabe flopped to the ground, crossing his legs. "So, is that the last bit of good news we're gonna have for a while?"

"I sure hope not," Torbon answered, plopping down beside him. "That would suck."

"Fortunately," Lina said, taking her own seat, nuzzled up alongside Torbon, "I think maybe this will provide us with some options...once I wrap my head around it."

"What is that?" Cabe asked.

Lina went through the same information she'd done with Taj, leaving the two men scratching their heads, wondering how they could take advantage of the device.

"I mean, that's slick and all, but even if you make it work, what can we do with it?" Torbon scratched at his scorched spot, leaning against the wall.

Lina shrugged. "Not sure yet, but there has to be some use. I'm not sure what all this stupid thing can do," she told them. "In theory, it controls the majority of the ship functions. In reality, what does that mean when the ship is a wreck and half its systems are shot?"

"Maybe we can seal the ship and shut off life support," Torbon offered, bolting upright, eyebrows raised.

"If there was anyone on the ship beside captives, and if all the aliens weren't wearing portable breathing devices, that might work," Taj answered.

Torbon sighed and dropped back against the wall.

"That's all I have for now. I think my brain got a little cooked when the shuttle's engines clipped me."

"As if it wasn't a little cooked before that," Cabe joked, grinning wide and clapping Torbon on the shoulder.

Torbon chuckled. "Yeah, maybe. Wish I had some nip to even it out, though."

"Me, too," Cabe agreed. "Gave the last I had to Mama." His face soured at the mention of the old Gran. Everyone's followed suit, and Taj sank into herself.

She felt like a failure, like she'd let Mama and Beaux down. "What would they do?" she muttered to herself.

"What would who do?" Lina asked.

Taj shook her head, only then realizing she'd asked the question aloud. "What would Mama and Gran Beaux do were they in this position?"

"Something bold and daring, off the wall and totally unexpected," Cabe answered.

"No pressure there, huh?"

"You asked," he replied, and Taj nodded.

"I did indeed."

"Maybe you should stop worrying about what the Grans would do and think about what *you'd* do," Lina told her. "Seems Beaux and Mama put you in charge. Gotta figure there was a reason for that. If they wanted clones of themselves, old blood, old ideas, they would have put one of the other Grans in place, one of the elders. Sounds to me like they wanted something, *someone*, different."

"So, just be me?" Taj asked.

"Exactly."

Taj chucked and *thumped* her back against the wall. "Sounds like a self-help slogan rather than a plan." She raised her hands in the air and shouted, "Be yourself and conquer the enemy!"

"Okay, maybe it does sound a bit like litter," Lina admitted.

Taj sighed and clambered to her feet. She tapped the side of her skull. "It all sounds like litter right now." A yawn slipped loose as she glanced down the corridor. "I think I'm gonna take a walk, clear my brain a little. Maybe I can figure out what possessed Beaux and Mama to put me in charge." She gave the crew a slim grin and waved, heading off before they could do much more than mutter goodbyes.

It wasn't that she didn't want to be around them, especially since Torbon was alive and well, but she needed some time alone. Her world had been spinning ever since the aliens crash-landed on the planet, and she hadn't had any time to really think, to process anything.

Her existence had been one huge reactionary blur, something thrown in her path every time she stopped to catch her breath. She needed a moment to herself, and as selfish as that felt given the circumstances, there was no way she'd be able to think straight if she didn't take it.

The end of the world would have to wait a moment.

She chuckled at her thought, listening to her feet scrape across the stone as she walked. Arms extended, she ran her fingertips along the rough-hewn walls, the cold seeping in the longer she traveled. She breathed in the musty dankness of the tunnels, letting the stale air fill her lungs. Unconsciously, she steered clear of the others in the tunnels and found herself trailing along the corridor that led toward the alien prisoner she'd blinded.

A pang of guilt struck her as she neared his alcove, and

she slowed as she came upon it. Grady was there, keeping watch. He grunted and nodded to her as she came to a halt outside the alcove.

"How's he doing?" she asked.

Grady shrugged. "Not bad for an alien prisoner of war. Seems to be pretty comfortable."

Taj sighed at the old man's attitude. "How about you take a break. I'll watch him."

The old Tom conceded with a grunt and walked off without a word. Taj waited until he was gone, then dropped to the floor outside the alcove.

"You ever wonder what's gonna happen next?" she asked the soldier.

He shook his head, the red palmprint on his chest gleaming in the dim light. "Not really," he answered. "Sooner or later, likely sooner, Captain Vort is going to find out where you're hiding, then he's going to send his entire force down here to wipe you out." He turned his head in her direction, and though his eyes were swollen, bloody messes, Taj felt a phantom stare landing on her.

"And me, too, of course," he added. "He won't discriminate. Of that, you can be sure. That mineral he's having everyone mine is worth more to him than anything. It's his ticket to being a hero, to his name being immortalized in the Wyyvan Empire as the man who found the means to take on the Federation."

Taj wanted to ask more about this Federation S'thlor spoke about, but after their last discussion, it was clear his biases were too volatile to see past. Still, she wondered if there was something in Lina's new toy that would offer a better idea as to who this so-called Federation was. Maybe they could help the Furlorians. Maybe Taj could find a way to reach out to them. If the Wyyvans hated them so much, maybe they could be put to use in Krawlas's defense.

S'thlor shifted and turned to face her, as best he could with his hands and legs bound. "All that at stake, you can guarantee Captain Vort will do everything he can to wipe you out," the alien told her. "He'll chase you to the end of the planet to make sure he kills each and every one of you."

Taj sighed and climbed to her feet, letting his words sink in. She stood quietly, processing, when a quiet chuckle broke free of her of its own accord. An ember of an idea sparked in her brain, flaring to life as if under a swift breeze. She grinned.

"You know, that might not be a bad thing at all."

S'thlor's face crinkled. "You're a strange creature, Furlorian," he said. "A madman willing to pursue you relentlessly to your death isn't usually something perceived as positive."

"Depends on how you look at it, I guess," she replied, not bothering to say more to the alien.

Taj called Grady back to his post, then darted down the hall, leaving the captive soldier behind as she went off in search of Lina.

She'd know soon enough if she was crazy or a genius.

Or a little of both.

Taj figured the latter, and she was okay with that.

CHAPTER TWENTY-SEVEN

Taj stared through the gazefinders at the gangplank of the *Monger*. Like before, two guards stood outside, pacing back and forth in bored monotony. The sun had yet to slither away, but it was close, casting long shadows over the alien craft.

"You sure about this?" Torbon asked.

Taj huffed. "I swear, the next person who asks me that question is gonna get shot." She snapped the gazefinders down and glared at Torbon, tapping her free hand on her holstered bolt pistol. "They won't need to wait for the enemy to come kill them."

He raised his hands in surrender. "All right, all right. Rowl," he muttered. "Sorry for trying to reassure myself."

She sighed, returning to her vigil. "I'm tired of the question, that's all. It's not like I know what the gack I'm doing here. Rowl, none of us do. There's no handbook for any of this, much as I wish there were."

"If only."

Taj sighed, twisting her neck in an effort to get it to loosen up. A sad, single *pop* was all she could manage. A quiet groan slipped out, and she cut it off as she spotted movement trundling toward the *Monger*'s gangplank. "There," she whispered out of instinct, though they were far enough from the ship to shout and not be heard. "There he is."

Torbon crouched closer to her, kicking up sand from the dune they shared, even though he couldn't possibly see what she saw through the gazefinders. She ignored his frantic movements and stared off into the distance, watching as the shadowy figure took shape and resolved.

The Wyyvan soldier stumbled forward, looking out of place in the brown desert with his black armor, a splash of red at the chest. He angled toward his two companions at the entryway to the destroyer, and they slowed and stared at him with awkward stances, weapons half-raised but lacking any real commitment or concern.

The alien staggered up to the others as Taj watched, his arms waving, then he stumbled to a short, jerky halt. He appeared to speak to the soldiers on duty, an animated conversation that looked entirely one-sided from where Taj looked on.

She wondered what was being said and strained to hear, despite knowing they were too far from her for that, but she couldn't help herself. Her breath hung stale in her lungs, and she waited, watching until she felt as if she might pass out. Then, at long last, the guard waved the other soldier inside, and the alien made his way up the gangplank in a rush, disappearing inside the ship.

Taj exhaled, letting the black dots in her vision fade before pulling the gazefinders aside. "He's in," she said.

Torbon nodded and flopped to the dirt, rolling onto his back with a sigh. "Here we go."

CHAPTER TWENTY-EIGHT

"Good news, Captain," Commander Dard said, an excited hitch in his voice. Vort heard his fist thump against his chest before the captain even managed to turn about.

"My favorite kind of news," he replied, spinning on a heel to face the commander. "What is it?"

"A Furlorian has broken, at last." Vort could almost see the grin behind Dard's visor it gleamed so brightly. He swayed side to side as if unable to contain his excitement. "She wishes to speak to you directly."

"Does she now?" Vort chuckled. "I think, perhaps, I can tolerate her presence long enough to extract that information." Vort straightened, gesturing for Dard to lead the way.

Dard started off, his heavy bootsteps clattering down the hallways until they reached the cells. He waved at the guard outside, who opened the outer door and ushered the pair inside.

Vort's visor fogged, atmospherics clearing it an instant later, but he was grateful for the breathing mask he wore. Judging by the wreckage splayed about the cells, it was clear Kabal had been at work, and Vort was glad not to have to smell the wretched stench of ruined bodies.

Dard led him to the centermost cage and motioned the ruin of a creature inside. It barely lifted its head to meet Vort's gaze.

"So, I am told you wish to share something with me," Vort told the alien. "What is it?"

"Ple-ease, lord, I beg mercy," the Furlorian mumbled, the words slow and thick like sludge. "Please."

Vort drew closer to the bars, grinning. "And mercy you shall have if you tell me where the rest of your kind have gone to ground."

The Furlorian gave the shallowest of nods, barely a tremor of movement. "Yes, for mer-cy, I'll t-tell you."

"Then, by all means, do so."

The Furlorian groaned and lifted herself onto her elbows, blood pooling below the scabby points. "Tu-unnels beneath the city," she spat out. "A h-hatch in the wreck… wreckage of the meeting…hall. Access to…them," she managed to say, at last, getting the words out as if each were heavy stones, the burden enormous. As soon as they were free, she slumped to the ground once more. "M-mercy." Crimson bubbles fluttered up from where her mouth had fallen into the puddle.

Vort grinned and savored the moment before turning his attention back to the shattered Furlorian. "Open the gate," he called out, and Dard unlocked the cage and swung the door open. "I am a man of my word, Furlorian. I promised mercy, and you shall have it."

Captain Vort stepped forward and pressed his boot against the back of the Furlorian's neck. The creature gasped as her face was pressed hard against the steel floor, then a quiet gurgle resounded. She twitched and spasmed, trying to rise, but Vort held her fast, her face buried in the puddle of her own blood.

Weak from torture, she barely struggled, defying that last breath for only a moment before she could hold back no longer. She went to draw air and only found blood. She gagged and choked, each breath drawing her in deeper.

Vort pressed harder, her skull creaking against the floor, and a tremor ran through the old Furlorian's body. Once, twice, and then she went still. Vort held his boot on her neck a moment longer, finally pulling it free with a bark of laughter.

"Thus mercy has been bestowed." He turned to face Dard, his hands clasped together in glee. "I want all of the men gathered and made ready to assault the last of these vile creatures."

"All of them, sir?"

"All of them," Vort answered. "Pull the mining crews and all but the smallest cadre of guards off the hostages. Leave the flight crew and Kabal to their work, but I want everyone else armed and ready to invade the secretive little tunnels the rats have been hiding in. We will slaughter them in a single push, and then we can get back to what's important, Commander." He grinned and slapped a hand on Dard's shoulder. "Our future."

Commander Dard saluted and issued the order. Vort trembled with excitement.

At last, the creatures would be wiped out, and Vort could revel in his find without the annoying buzz of rebellious insects.

The future called to him, and Vort made ready to answer.

CHAPTER TWENTY-NINE

Taj clung to her bolt pistol, feeling the sweat of her palms make it loose in her hand.

She hated waiting.

"Are you sure—" Cabe started, but Taj cut him off, shoving the barrel of her bolt pistol against his cheek.

"You guys never listen, do you?" she asked.

Cabe stared at her with round eyes, gleaming with moisture. He pushed the gun aside. "Rowl, Taj. I was gonna—"

"Seriously, don't ask if I'm sure about this," she told him, shaking her head. "You and Torbon, I swear." She wiped the back of her hand across her brow, smearing more sweat than wiping it away. Ears pinned back alongside her head, she glanced upward at the heavy steel hatch above. "I'll be sure when that hatch opens."

"Fair enough," he muttered, shaking his head. He clung to his own pistol, not looking any more comfortable holding it than she did. "How long do we have?"

She shrugged. "No idea."

"Then I guess I better not wait," he said.

Before she could ask what he meant, Cabe darted forward and planted a kiss on her, pulling her in tight with his free hand. Taj gasped, caught off guard, but the gentle tingle that ran along her scruff and set it alight kept her from pulling away. Instead, she leaned in harder, savoring the kiss and closeness.

Given what she'd set in motion, she had no clue when she might get to hold Cabe so closely again, to have him all to herself again. *Might be never,* she thought, immediately regretting the thought, however true it might be. Still, at that moment, he was all hers.

At least until a sudden thump echoed above, and the hatch was flung open, dim light stabbing down toward them.

"It's here," an alien called out, peering over the edge of the hatch.

Taj grunted, broke loose of Cabe, and shot the alien in his face. "Now I'm sure," she shouted, then shot off into the tunnels, Cabe at her side.

"Get them," she heard someone scream, the voice too familiar to be anyone but the alien captain himself. Then she heard the sullen *thump* of armored soldiers spilling into the tunnels at their back.

Taj hunkered down and ran even faster, death on their heels.

CHAPTER THIRTY

C aptain Vort thrilled behind his visor, watching as his soldiers poured into the secretive hatch inside the burnt-out building.

At first, he'd been furious to learn the rodents had been hiding right beneath his feet this entire time, but once his fury calmed, he realized it was best for him that they were so close, so easily reached. It meant he wouldn't have to spend much time mobilizing his forces to take them out. A few short meters beneath them, he could press his attack right away and ensure that each and every one of the locals felt his wrath.

"Kill them all," he ordered, envisioning the piles of bodies his men would have to burn out in the fields.

Better still, he couldn't wait until the locals were slaughtered so he could tour those very same tunnels for opportunity. If nothing else, he could use them to hide personal cache of Toradium-42 from the empire, using a section of the labyrinth as his private vault.

He grinned and urged his men on, his heart pounding against his ribs. Soon, it would be all over, and Vort would be so much more than a captain.

CHAPTER THIRTY-ONE

Taj gasped and stumbled to a halt, her breath catching in her lungs. Her eyes scanned the gloomy tunnel, head on a swivel, as the sound of pursuing aliens continued behind her as if building a sparkstorm.

"Where is it?" Cabe asked, similarly out of breath. He looked pale, frazzled, tufts of fur sticking out in every direction.

Taj didn't waste air answering. She pushed on, running her hands along the walls and doing her best to catch a familiar scent. Then, after a moment where she was ready to collapse, to give in to despair, she caught sight of what she'd been looking for.

"There!"

She raced a few meters farther down the tunnel and sighed loudly as her hand clasped over the roughened rung of a rope ladder. It dangled from a slightly-opened hatch above.

"Oh, praise Rowl," Cabe muttered, coming up behind her, urging her on.

Taj steeled the last of her strength and started up the ladder. Right then, the hatch popped open, and a visored helmet appeared, staring down at them. Taj's pulse raced, adrenaline setting fire to her veins. She swung precariously from the ladder by one hand as she pawed at her bolt pistol, yanking it from its holster.

"Whoa!" the soldier shouted. He rose up, hands raised, fumbling at his helmet. The visor slid away, and behind its darkened screen, Taj spied Torbon's grinning face. "I'm on your side, remember?"

Taj growled. "Not dressed like that you aren't." She stuffed her pistol back in its holster and clambered the rest of the way up the ladder and out into the warm desert air. Torbon helped pull her from the tunnels, and she, in turn, helped Cabe scramble loose of their confines.

Cabe took one look at Torbon, dressed in the alien battle armor, a gleam of red smeared across his chest, and shook his head. "Damn near gave us heart attacks," he told him. "Why are you suited up like that?"

Torbon shrugged. "Figured I'd give it a try, see how the stuff fits. Kinda loose," he said, wiggling and showing how the armor rattled a bit on his slim frame. "Not sure how these guys wear this stuff all the time."

Taj tapped him on the skull. "We don't have time for this," she muttered. "Mind getting to work before we're overrun by a bunch of pissed-off aliens?"

Snapping to attention, he offered her a sharp salute. "Yes, sir," he said with a grin. "On it."

Before Taj could say more, he unsnapped two of the

silver grenades from his belt and activated them, tossing them in through the hatch.

"Fire in the hole," he shouted, chuckling as he kicked the hatch closed behind them. Cabe slammed the locks into place, and the crew darted away from the hatch. A moment later, two distinct explosions sounded, and the ground rumbled, kicking up a storm of dust.

Taj sighed, staring at the metal hatch as smoke squeezed its way between the seals. She stood there, silent a moment, before turning back to Torbon. "Tell Lina it's her turn. We don't have a lot of time."

Torbon, slapped the repaired visor on the alien helmet shut and raced off, clattering. Taj watched him go. It wasn't until he was gone that her thoughts settled, and she spotted the milling group of Furlorians in the distance, gathered behind a nearby dune. Several eyes watched her and Cabe, and she cast a nod in Grady's direction as he grinned at her.

"We get everyone?" she asked.

Cabe nodded. "Yup. Now we need to get them out of here."

Taj started off, casting furtive glances at the sky over her shoulder. "Then let's do that," she said, waving her people on. Grady passed the word, and the clustered people of Krawlas, weary and worn, marched alongside her in a tight circle.

Unlike the others, those captured and subjugated by Captain Vort and his soldiers, they did so with their chins raised, eyes defiant.

CHAPTER THIRTY-TWO

Vort stood in the town square. His men had long ago flooded the tunnels beneath the Furlorian city, and he waited impatiently for word as to their success. Each and every second was torture.

Until he saw the corpses of his enemies splayed out before him, he knew he would fret and fume, wanting nothing more than the total annihilation of the local resistance.

He paced back and forth near the hatch where his men had descended, kicking up debris as he carved a path in the wreckage. Over and over, he tapped his comm for updates only to be told the tunnel system was extensive, and his men were scouring every inch, rooting out the enemy. In fact, he'd heard the same response so many times he could repeat it verbatim.

He'd triggered the comm once more when Commander Dard coughed to get his attention.

"Sir?"

Vort waved him off, focused on the battle being waged beneath his feet. He was half-tempted to slip through the hatch himself and join the fight to hurry it along. How long did it take to root out exhausted, barely-armed rats?

"Sir!"

Vort growled, spinning on his commander. "What is it? Can't you see I'm busy?"

Commander Dard simply pointed in reply, drawing Vort's attention from his thoughts and settling it squarely on the object that had so thoroughly caught the commander's focus.

Captain Vort gasped before he could rein his reaction in. "What the hell are they doing?" he shouted, clanging his hands on his hips.

There, in the outskirts of Culvert City, the *Monger's* engines sputtered and flared, and the ship rose unsteadily in the air. In its wake, shadows swallowed the square, the roar of its passage growing steadily as it drifted upward, rising higher and higher.

"I didn't order this!" Vort cursed, whirling on Dard. "Bring them down now!"

The commander grunted. "Communications are down, Captain. I'm unable to reach the crew."

Captain Vort shrieked, stomping about in a circle. "I'll have each and every one of the crew tortured for this!" he screamed, waving a fist at the ship as it continued its ascent.

It was then that he noticed the gangplank remained open, the ship's primitive landing gear still jutting from beneath the *Monger's* hull. Then the engines flared, coughing blackness, before nearly giving out.

"What are they doing?" he asked. He glared at the ship, willing his gaze to pierce its hull so he could see into the bridge to determine what his wayward men were up to.

"Uh," Dard started, reaching over and clasping ahold of Vort's armor at the shoulder, "I think we need to move, sir."

"Why?" Vort shouted, knocking Dard's hand aside and spinning about to stare face-to-face with his officer. "What do you know, Commander? What are my men doing?"

Vort heard Dard swallow over the comm. "I don't think it's your men, Captain." He pointed at the ship once more, and Vort followed his finger.

The *Monger*'s engines flared once more, nearly burning out, and the ship's nose angled sharply, aimed toward the ground and the city. Toward them.

"Oh…" Vort muttered as the ship—*his* ship—shot forward, diving and cleaving through the air like a missile.

The captain swallowed hard as realization struck home, at last. This wasn't some errant crew failure. It was an attack.

An attack on him.

"Run!" he screamed, racing toward the desert with all the speed he could muster, Commander Dard on his heels.

CHAPTER THIRTY-THREE

Taj and Cabe watched as the *Monger* streaked toward Culvert City. Torn, she fought to keep her breathing calm as the plan she'd put in motion ran its course.

Somewhere deeper in the desert, Lina sat with Torbon and fiddled with the control cube she'd stolen from the great destroyer. She'd managed to interpret the basic function of it quickly and had realized she could take control of the flight system after Taj asked her about it specifically.

She grinned and thanked S'thlor for his unintended wisdom. It was his comment that had set all this in motion, his insight into Captain Vort. And the captive alien had been right. Vort would stop at nothing to rid himself of the Furlorians, and that meant marching his troops into a tight warren of tunnels with only a few exits and no way to quickly retreat.

Her stomach churned at the idea of what was about to happen, but this was war, she reminded herself. People died so others could live. Much as it bothered her to realize she was condemning hundreds of alien soldiers to their doom, it raised her spirits to know she was saving her own people in the process. It was a horrible sacrifice, but it was one she was willing to make.

Mama Merr and Beaux would be proud of her, she knew.

Then it was too late for anything but recriminations.

The *Monger*'s engine flared one last time, gathering as much speed as it could muster, and crashed into town, directly over the labyrinth of tunnels that had kept Taj's people safe for so long.

The ground rumbled, even as far away as Taj stood, watching the crash through her gazefinders, and she was nearly knocked off her feet. The *Monger* slammed into the earth and sank beneath, its momentum driving it deeper and deeper. Buildings toppled and fell into the crater the ship made, and Taj saw flashes of orange and red as the ship crumpled and its hull gave way.

While Lina hadn't been able to repair or control the weapon's system, she had been able to open all the bulkheads between the ship and the weapons store. Plasma torpedoes, no longer stabilized within their own compartments, exploded, setting off a chain reaction of great rippling explosions traveling the length of the *Monger*. Flames burst through the compromised hull, and fire jetted from thousands of newly-made vents. Death spilled into the tunnels, charring everything into ash in an instant.

Taj sighed. At least the soldiers' deaths had been quick, if not entirely painless.

It was hardly a consolation, but it was all she had.

She looked away, unable to watch any longer. More

than the idea that she'd condemned hundreds of men to death, she'd also killed Culvert City, burying them both together in a ruinous grave.

Everything she'd ever known was going up in flames. Every building, every place she'd played, her home, the homes of her friends, all gone in a flash, annihilated by the culmination of her idea.

Her stomach soured, and her earlier thoughts of Mama and Beaux being proud faded like Culvert City, going up in flames. How could they be proud of this?

As if reading her mind, Cabe set a hand on her shoulder. "All of this can be rebuilt," he told her. "Our people are safe, though, and that's all that matters."

Taj nodded, but still, she couldn't rid herself of the horror splayed out before her, the ruin she'd wrought upon her people. At least, right then, she could rationalize it as something that needed to be done, even if that didn't make her feel better about it.

"It's over," Cabe told her, pulling her in tighter.

She shook her head and let out a tired sigh, turning away from the wreckage of Culvert City. "No, it's not over yet," she said, breaking loose of Cabe and walking off. "We've one last loose end to tie up."

CHAPTER THIRTY-FOUR

After gathering the whole of the surviving Furlorians, from the barn and elsewhere, Taj led them around the city, each armed with whatever weapons they had at hand. *Not that it matters,* she thought, the slimmest of grins peeling her lips back.

The throng circled the glowing wreckage of their homes until they came across what they were looking for. The quiet shuffle of feet and weary souls turned raucous as they did.

"Well, well, well," Taj started, "what have we here?"

Captain Vort and Commander Dard stumbled through the desert, desperate to find cover, shelter, someplace to hide. They'd had no luck with the whole of the Furlorian population sussing them out before either had a chance to find sanctuary in the unforgiving land.

Vort stiffened. He reached instinctively for Dard's blaster pistol, but the commander was faster. He drew the weapon and tossed it aside as nearly two hundred Furlorians clustered around them.

Vort glared, the piercing dots of his eyes visible even behind his visor, but he said nothing, likely realizing his commander had been right in ridding himself of the weapon. It would do them no good anyway.

Taj and the crew split the crowd apart and approached the pair, who stiffened in place and held their ground without a word. Judgment had come to call, and both knew the scales were against them.

"Now, what to do with you two?" Taj said, holding the barrel of her bolt pistol on them. Dozens of other weapons were trained on the aliens similarly, assuring Taj there would be no escape from their fate no matter what the two enemies might try. "I suppose I should shoot you after all you've done."

Dard groaned and dropped to his knees. Vort held his ground, easing a hand upward to lift his visor. The greenish hue of his skin seemed sickly in the glowing embers of Culvert City.

"I am a valuable man," he told the assemblage, "important. My masters would pay you an emperor's ransom in exchange for me."

Taj let loose a bark of laughter. "I doubt that, Captain," she answered, gesturing over her shoulder to where Private S'thlor stood among the gathered Furlorians. "I know all about your society and how little it values anything but itself. Your admiral won't pay for your release, nor would he waste a moment contemplating it." She shook her head. "No, you have no value to him or your people, so don't waste my time."

"But...but..."

"But nothing, Captain," she said, stepping forward and pressing the barrel of her pistol to his head. "Fortunately for you, however, you *do* have some value to me as an informant." Taj offered him a crooked grin. "So, here are your options, Captain. Surrender peacefully and avail yourself to my questions whenever I think to ask them or die here on your knees. The choice is yours."

Torbon kicked the captain's legs out from under him, driving him to the dirt alongside Commander Dard.

"What say you, Captain Vort?" Taj asked. "Live or die?"

Vort cast a furtive glance over at Dard and let out a loud sigh, shifting his gaze back to Taj. "I choose to live, of course."

Taj chuckled and holstered her pistol. "Then that's settled." She waved to her crew, and Torbon and Cabe secured the prisoners and helped them to their feet. "Find somewhere safe to keep these two until I decide I have some use for them."

The two aliens were hauled away in silence. Once they were gone, Taj addressed the crowd. "I know this is a bittersweet victory, everything we've ever known razed and burning over there," she motioned toward Culvert City, "but we're alive. Mama Merr and Gran Beaux would consider that a win."

"Hear, hear!" Grady shouted, mustering the crowd behind him. Cheers erupted.

Taj waited them out, letting the people—*her* people— revel in the moment before she ruined it with the cold hard truth of their future. At last, after they'd settled, she raised her hands to ensure she had their full attention once more.

"Unfortunately, this was the first battle in the coming war." Her words were met with stoic silence. "Our dear captain back there—" she gestured in the general direction the crew had taken the enemy commanders "—has reached out to his people and made it clear Krawlas harbors a means to an end in their war against their Federation enemy. They will not simply leave us be or pass us by. And though we have no knowledge of when the alien's call for assistance might be answered, we can be absolutely certain it will be. They will come for us, but we will be ready this time, prepared."

Lina came over, holding up the control cube she'd scavenged from the Monger. Taj gestured to the device.

"This thing contains a clone of every database aboard the enemy destroyer, to include technical specs and communication protocols. With it, we have the means to face our enemy on even terms. That is," she said, letting her words drag out into sobering pause, "if you're willing to fight."

The crowd roared, and Taj grinned in response to their enthusiasm.

Let them come, she thought. *We'll be ready.*

EPILOGUE

Taj stared out at the shell of the newly reborn Culvert City and smiled. As different as it looked, still, there was no mistaking it as anything but home.

She watched as her people flitted about, working here and there in their efforts to rebuild their day to day lives. It was a satisfying view, seeing everyone doing their part to remake Furlorian society.

Even more satisfying was what Taj couldn't see.

With the grudging help of Captain Vort and Commander Dard, and the continued expansion of knowledge gained by Lina's efforts with the control cube, the Furlorians were becoming more than prepared.

They'd learned to manipulate the Toradium-42 to refuel the Paradigm, readying it for travel once more. They'd also scavenged a number of operational weapons from the wreck of the *Monger*, transferring those to the *Paradigm* to provide her with the barest of defensive capabilities.

Taj grinned, picturing the great old ship in the sky once more. It had been so long since she'd seen it.

But there was more to Taj's smile than nostalgia. The Toradium-42 had several uses, and she and her people were in the process of making the most of its properties, readying for the inevitable day when more Wyyvan invaders would descend upon Krawlas in an attempt to subjugate and lay waste to the Furlorian people.

To their dismay, they'd find a far different enemy standing against them this time.

AUTHOR NOTES - TIM MARQUITZ

WRITTEN JUNE 19, 2018

Thanks for picking up my first foray into the Kurtherian Gambit Universe, Age of Expansion. You're the reason I get to do what I love every day, and I appreciate every moment of it. Looking forward to sharing this adventure with you and can't wait to hear your thoughts. Thank you!

Thanks to Craig Martelle and Michael Anderle for giving me the opportunity to run amok in their playground. And thanks to all the folks at LMBPN for making this a great experience.

Special thanks go out to the LMBPN Beta Readers and the JIT team. You guys rock.

(Craig Martelle, standing in – this message was approved by MA)

Woohoo! You're still reading because you are awesome! We wouldn't be anywhere without fans, those good people who buy our books or borrow them through Kindle Unlimited and read them. You are the absolute best. Thank you. If you can also drop us a review on Amazon, that is icing on the virtual cake.

Michael and I talked about these author notes as he asked me to write them on his behalf since he is swamped with other stuff. I said no problem at all, even after a back and forth of cursing that ended with "Ass."

I don't even know what we were talking about at that point, but it sure as hell wasn't Enemy of my Enemy, which is an outstanding addition to the Kurtherian Gambit Universe.

I met Tim Marquitz online well over two years ago. Tim introduced me to Monique who signed me as part of a traditional publishing contract. I went on to write four books with Permuted Press. Tim was heavy into his Demon Squad series and if you haven't read that, you need to get on that right away. I knew he would be a great fit for this universe, so I begged him over a long period to come on board. It only cost us a Ferrari delivered to his house and the passenger seat filled with cash to get him to write this series.

Okay. There was no Ferrari. I can hear Michael now – "Why are you talking about a Ferrari? Old dudes can't get into them. It's like sitting on the ground. How about a nice Bentley?" I digress.

Tim writes great characters with a passion for life. He makes them three dimensional and makes the reader care about them. There is no higher testimonial for an author. Anything well-described loses luster if we don't care about the characters.

Welcome aboard, Tim! This is going to be a great ride. I love your characters and your story and think that the fans will, too. Your fans will become our fans and we hope that ours become yours.

Tim came to Vegas last year for the 20Books Vegas 2017 conference. I'd like to think he had a great time, talking with a wide variety of other authors and most importantly, he got to spend time with Michael and me. We clicked because he's a professional, just like us.

Tim has a beard. It's long and white. He may be a wizard. I can't be sure.

There is more to come. This is the first in a three-book arc that could easily be ten books. The first three covers are by Tom Edwards, who has done about twenty covers for me. I couldn't be happier to get Tom's work on some KGU stories. The fans deserve the best and Tom is.

Tom doesn't have a beard. And he's English, so you can tell him apart from Tim and me. He's also a bit younger than us old guys. Once again, I digress.

Tim Marquitz. Author extraordinaire. On board the KGU train, adding momentum to an already great bunch of series. Well done, Tim! I look forward to your second and third books.

Semper Fi, my friends, or as Michael would say, Ad Aeternitatem.

Craig Martelle

BOOKS BY TIM MARQUITZ

Also Available from Tim Marquitz

The Demon Squad Series

From Hell (Novella)
DS1 - Armageddon Bound
DS2 - Resurrection
Betrayal (Intro short to At the Gates)
DS3 - At the Gates
DS4 - Echoes of the Past
DS5 - Beyond the Veil
DS6 - The Best of Enemies
DS7 - Exit Wounds
DS8 - Collateral Damage
DS9 – Aftermath
DS10 – Institutionalized
To Hell and Back - A Demon Squad Collection (books 1-3)

The Blood War Trilogy

Dawn of War
Embers of an Age
Requiem

Clandestine Daze Series

Eyes Deep (novella)
Influx

Standalone Fantasy

Dirge
Witch Bane
War God Rising

Sci-fi

Excalibur

Dead West

Those Poor, Poor Bastards
The Ten Thousand Things
Omnibus 1

Horror

Prey
Serial

Skulls
Heir to the Blood Throne: Inheritance

Collections

Tales of Magic and Misery

Non-Fiction

Memoirs of a Machine – w/John MACHINE Lober
Grunt Style: The Blue Collar Guide to Writing Genre
Fiction

Anthologies

Blackguards (Ragnarok Publications)
Unbound (Grim Oak Press)
SNAFU: Survival of the Fittest (Cohesion Press)
SNAFU: Hunters (Cohesion Press)
SNAFU: Future Warfare (Cohesion Press)
SNAFU: Black Ops (Cohesion Press)
In the Shadow of the Towers (Night Shade)
Neverland's Library (Ragnarok Publications)
At Hell's Gates 1&3 (Charity)
American Nightmare (Kraken Press)
Corrupts Absolutely? (Ragnarok Publications)
Widowmakers (Charity)
That Hoodoo Voodoo, That You Do (Ragnarok
Publications)

BOOKS BY MICHAEL ANDERLE

For a complete list of books by Michael Anderle, please visit:

www.lmbpn.com/ma-books/

All LMBPN Audiobooks are Available at Audible.com and iTunes

To see all LMBPN audiobooks, including those written by
Michael Anderle please visit:

www.lmbpn.com/audible

Craig Martelle's other books (listed by series)

Terry Henry Walton Chronicles (co-written with Michael Anderle) – a post-apocalyptic paranormal adventure

Gateway to the Universe (co-written with Justin Sloan & Michael Anderle) – this book transitions the characters from the Terry Henry Walton Chronicles to The Bad Company

The Bad Company (co-written with Michael Anderle) – a military science fiction space opera

End Times Alaska (also available in audio) – a Permuted Press publication – a post-apocalyptic survivalist adventure

The Free Trader – a Young Adult Science Fiction Action Adventure

Cygnus Space Opera – A Young Adult Space Opera (set in the Free Trader universe)

Darklanding (co-written with Scott Moon) – a Space Western

Rick Banik – Spy & Terrorism Action Adventure

Become a Successful Indie Author – a non-fiction work

About Tim Marquitz

Tim Marquitz is the author of the Demon Squad series, the Blood War Trilogy, co-author of the Dead West series, as well as several standalone books, and numerous anthology appearances. Tim also collaborated on Memoirs of a MACHINE, the story of MMA pioneer John Machine Lober.

Website: www.tmarquitz.com

Follow Tim on Facebook and Twitter.

Subscribe to Tim's newsletter and get up to date information on new releases as well as an Excalibur prequel story (exciting sci-fi) and Dawn of War, the first novel in the Blood War Trilogy (Epic Fantasy)!

http://www.tmarquitz.com/contact

Michael Anderle Social

Website: http://kurtherianbooks.com/

Email List: http://kurtherianbooks.com/email-list/
Facebook:
https://www.facebook.com/TheKurtherianGambitBoo
ks/

Craig Martelle Social

Website & Newsletter:
http://www.craigmartelle.com

Facebook:
https://www.facebook.com/AuthorCraigMartelle/